Murder &
The Money Pit

Renee George

Murder & The Money Pit

(Barkside of the Moon Mysteries Book 2)

ISBN-13: 978-1-947177-17-8

Pit Bulls are Sweet . . .and that's no mystery!

Sometimes, trying to be part of the human world can be a real killer. . . Cougar-shifter Lily Mason is ready to put down roots in the human town of Moonrise, Missouri. She only has two problems: her attraction and proximity to Parker Knowles, her boss at the Pit Bull Rescue Shelter, and her need to shift into animal form more than once a month.

When she gets the opportunity to buy a "fixer-upper" outside of Moonrise with plenty of room to get wild without running into easily freaked-out humans, Lily jumps at the chance. Smooshie, Lily's lovable pit bull and partner in chaos, is eager to participate with the home improvements. Unfortunately, Smooshie's help includes digging out a mummified body from the living room wall.

Lily is still recovering from the last murder investigation she got involved in–and she's not looking forward to being in the middle of another one. The case gets even stickier when Lily's landlord is murdered, rumors of a heist gone wrong run rampant, and Parker's old high school buddies have returned to Moonrise, thus increasing the suspect pool. Lily's attempts to become a bona fide citizen of Moonrise might well be thwarted by this newest complication–especially when the murderer sets sights on her.

DEDICATION

For Steve, Taylor, Josie, Kona, Simon, and Ash. You are the best Forever Family ever.

CONTENTS

ACKNOWLEDGMENTS

First, I have to thank **Lauren Allen** of the **Missouri Pit Bull Rescue** organization for patiently answering each one of my questions about pit bull rescue (no matter how crazy they might have been). Thank you for sharing the stories of success and failure you all experience in your quest to save this wonderful breed. I encourage everyone who loves dogs to donate to this group (www.mopitbullrescue.org) as they build their new shelter that will allow them to house even more rescues until they can be placed in foster or forever homes. The shelter in my book is more well-funded than real life shelters, but that is the benefit of fiction. There is not nearly enough money, volunteers, or space at most of these places to help all the pit bulls who need to be rescued. Any mistakes I may have written about "pit bull rescue" are mine and mine alone.

Second, I have to thank the usual suspects, Michele Bardsley and Robbin Clubb. You two get me through it. Every. Time. Whew. And this book is so much better because of you both.

Third, to my editor Kelli Collins (editmethis.com), thank the Goddess for you! You are the grammar and content ninja!

Last, I want to thank coffee for keeping me going. Thank you, Coffee. Thank you, thank you.

CHAPTER ONE

I HAVE NEVER been an impulsive person. I look both ways before crossing the street, I test the water with my toe before wading in, and I don't buy dilapidated, two-story rural houses.

Oh, wait. Yes, I do. The decrepit home on twelve acres of wooded land outside Moonrise, Missouri, was mine-ish. I'd just signed an "as is" rent-to-own, fifteen-year contract with Merl Peterson, a property developer, and had given him a ten grand down payment.

What have you done, Lily Mason?

"The place needs a lot of work," Merl said. His bushy eyebrows were as thick and long as the hair on his head was thin and short. "It hasn't had any work done on it in a long time. I was planning to fix it up myself for a cushy resale price, but Greer's a hard man to say no to."

"Greer's a good man," I said. "One of the best."

Greer Knowles was a mechanic in Moonrise. He owned a small garage called The Rusty Wrench. He was the very first person I met when I came to town, thanks to my green and yellow mini-truck, aka the rust bucket. I've had the truck for over twenty years now, and Martha, even with her occasional problems, was still the most reliable thing in my life. At least, she'd been the most consistent. I looked over at her. Martha's wheel well rust had gotten worse over the winter. Salted roads had a tendency to speed up oxidation. But lucky for me, Greer knew how to keep her in top running order.

Greer was also the father of my boss and friend, Parker.

My heart picked up the pace, the way it always did when I thought of Parker. I was currently living over his garage in a small studio apartment. As much as I wanted independence and a place of my own, another reason this house was so important to me was because I needed distance from Parker. It was hard working with a man I had feelings for when I knew nothing could ever come from them. Living right next to him made my heartache almost unbearable.

Merl pushed up his thick glasses and shook his head. "I have another place in town that's cheaper if this doesn't suit you."

What Merl didn't understand was that I liked the tall columns out on the porch and the ornate gables. There was something about this house, a certain charm, that I wanted to preserve. To make mine. Besides, my pit bull Smooshie needed room to run, to be free to stretch her thick legs. Frankly, I needed the same. As a werecougar living in a human town, I didn't often have the privacy needed to shift.

Smooshie barked and yipped with manic energy. I looked over in time to see my eighty-pound brown and white pittie leaping around after an orange and black Monarch butterfly near a patch of milkweed. We'd had a warm end to winter, and spring was a couple of weeks away. Even so, seeing a butterfly this early in March was unusual. Smooshie leaped again, her whole body twisting in the air.

I smiled. I really loved that dog.

"I'll be fine, Mr. Peterson. I have plans for the place."

"I hope a bulldozer's involved," he muttered.

I didn't say "what?" because I'd heard him loud and clear. My excellent hearing was the blessing and curse of being a cougar Shifter. I could also smell the remnants of his lunch—a burger with bacon, grilled onions, and bleu cheese. Buying a house on an empty stomach was no bueno. I turned to him and said, "Thank you, Mr. Peterson. I appreciate you taking a chance on me."

"Greer says you're okay, then you're okay in my book." The older man smiled, the lines around his eyes crinkling into small canyons. "Don't mind the ghosts." He grinned now.

Parker had tried to talk me out of the place. He'd said it was haunted. His expression had been so severe that I'd tried not to laugh. Not because I didn't believe in ghosts, quite the contrary. It's just that I grew up in a town with way scarier paranormal creatures than spirits. Besides, the ghost angle had allowed me to get the place at a steal. No one wanted to live in a house where people disappeared and were never seen from again. Except me.

"If it's all right, I'd like to hang out for a while, just to get some ideas and stuff," I told Merl.

"Sure," he said. "I'll have Jock Simmons send you copies of the contract. We'll get things finalized this week."

"It's okay that I get the trailer moved over and stuff now, right?"

"Of course. The place is yours. Just need to dot the i's and cross the t's, but as far as I'm concerned, you are home."

I smiled. "Sounds good." When Merl left, I pulled out my phone and made a call. "Haze. I got the house," I said when my BFF answered.

"Oh. Em. Gee!" She materialized and hugged me hard. "That's amazing."

Smooshie's barking grew even more excited, almost verging on a frantic hysteria as she danced around Hazel, going up on two feet, but not quite jumping on her.

"Will you muzzle your beast?" a squeaky voice demanded. A red squirrel climbed Haze to get away from my pittie.

"She's just saying hello, Tiz." I scratched Smooshie behind the ear, and she leaned her thick body into me, her tail whacking the back of my thighs as she panted her pleasure.

Hazel Kinsey is a witch, and Tizzy, a squirrel, is her familiar. They were both my best and only friends when I was growing up. Being short and skinny in a Shifter community was the same as being weak and useless. I'd never wanted to stay in Paradise Falls, but the death of my parents had made that choice for me. I'd had to drop out of high school to support my little brother, and I stayed until he died. It still hurt to think of Danny. There was nothing left for me there once he was gone.

"Is this it?" Tizzy asked. She made a chittering sound of disgust. "What a dump."

"Tiz!" Haze crossed her arms. "It just needs a little TLC. And maybe a little..." She wiggled her fingers.

"No magic," I said.

"Not even a little?"

"She's probably worried you'll blow her house down." Tizzy jumped to my shoulder. "Not that it would take much. Did you find this place in Deader Homes and Gardens?"

"Ha ha. Very funny."

"I thought so." Tizzy pulled an almond from somewhere on her furry person—I didn't want to know from where—and began to chew. "I like all the trees. And oh, look! Squirrels." Two gray squirrels ran up a mature maple. I rolled my eyes.

Haze, who was taller than me by six inches, put her arm around my shoulders. "You'll make it a real home, Lily. I have every faith."

"Thanks for lending me the down payment."

She smiled. "I know you're good for it." She gave me a squeeze.

"I'm kind of scared, Haze."

My BFF put her hands on my shoulders and stared down at me. "Why?"

"I'm not sure I can make it out here." By "out here" I meant in an entirely human town. Well, mostly. I'd never had to hide before, and I wasn't sure I could keep it up. "Aside from the fact that I'm a fish out of water—"

"More like a cat out of the litter box," Tizzy snarked.

I ignored her. "I didn't even finish high school. I don't make enough working at the shelter to afford a mortgage and food." Shifters burned through calories like fire burned through a month-old Christmas tree. And I needed a lot of protein in my diet, too. "Have you checked out the price of beef lately? It's ridiculous. I could spend a paycheck on red meat alone."

"Have you thought about getting your GED, maybe taking some classes at the local college?"

"I don't know."

"You're the smartest person I know, Lily Mason. It would be a shame to let all those brains go to waste."

Hazel believed every word she said. I could smell the truth on her. It was a gift passed down from my great-great-grandmother on my mother's side, who happened to be a witch, amazingly enough. I only found out in October that I wasn't pure Shifter, and some dangerous magic back home had triggered my ability as a truth-sayer. Most people wanted to be truthful, anyhow, and my power allowed them to open up to me. It didn't always work. If someone wanted to hide a secret bad enough, they could resist the compulsion to come clean.

I nodded to my friend. "I won't give up."

"Good, because you've been happy here, Lils. More happy than I'd ever seen you before." She squeezed my shoulders. "Humans are good for you."

"Yeah, yeah." I could hear the roar of a dually truck engine less than a mile away. "My boss is coming. You better get out of here."

"The boss?" She made *the* sound like *thee*. "The one who basically rescued you and swept you off your feet?"

"Stop," I said. "Seriously. You need to go."

Haze's phone played "Bear Necessities" from *The Jungle Book*. "Shoot, that's Ford." She looked at the screen. "It's a 9-1-1. There's been trouble since Halloween between the Shifters and the witches, and with spring right around the corner, it's not getting any better." She kissed my cheek. "Call me if you need me."

"I'll be fine," I told her and gave her a quick hug.

"Bye, Lils!" Tizzy said as she circled her witch's waist and climbed up her back. "Next time leave your beast at home."

I knelt next to Smooshie, who happily wagged. "She is home."

Tizzy stuck her tiny tongue out at me. Haze gave me a wistful smile. "Tell lover boy I said hello."

"He's not—" They disappeared before I could finish my protest. Parker's big black truck was throwing dust up as it came down the gravel drive.

The truck ground to a halt about thirty feet away. Parker rubbed his hand over his dark hair before he opened the driver-side door and stepped out. He was average height, about five feet eleven inches, which was still eight inches taller than me. I'd always been a bit of a runt. He had a broad chest, muscular arms, and crystal-blue eyes that nearly undid me every time he looked my way.

His dog Elvis—half pit bull, half horse—jumped out of the truck after him. The large, silvery-blue beauty hugged his body against his master's legs. As a PTSD dog, Elvis had been trained to pick up on Parker's body language and put himself between Parker and stressors. Turns out I was one of those stressors. I didn't want to make Parker's life difficult. Just the opposite. It was the reason I needed my own place.

"Whatcha doing out here?" I asked, shielding my eyes from the sun as he approached. An easy breeze carried his scent to me, and I fought the urge to run into his arms. We were friends. Nothing more. No matter what my Shifter libido wanted.

"I have to run into Cape Girardeau for some supplies, and dad asked me to bring you out his toolbox, shovel, and plaster scraper." He reached into the bed of the truck and lifted out a red bifold-topped metal box.

"It's so I can bury the bodies."

Parker froze for a moment. A crooked smile played on his lips. "You need help? I got a hacksaw back home."

I laughed. "These will do." I took the shovel and scraper from him. I followed him to the porch where he set the toolbox down.

"There you go," Parker said. He rubbed his hands on his jeans and put them in the pockets of his windbreaker.

"Tell Greer I owe him some pie." It was a joke between us. Parker's dad and I shared a love of food in a pastry.

"I'll let him know." His low voice always made my stomach jittery.

Smooshie and Elvis sniffed each other, with Smooshie getting her full nose right up his butt. I didn't want to begrudge her the formal dog greeting of an old friend, but automatically, I said, "Stop that."

Smooshie cocked her head at me, gave Elvis one more nose goose then moved away. Thank heavens Elvis tolerated Smooshie. He outweighed her by at least thirty pounds.

"You sure you want to live out here?" Parker asked. "It's going to take a lot of work to get this place livable."

"Buzz is moving in with Nadine. He's going to let me put his trailer out here to live in until I can get it all fixed up."

Buzz was actually my uncle and was a good forty years older than me, but since we were both Shifters, we could pass for nearly the same age.

Nadine was one of the few friends I'd made since I moved to Moonrise. She was a deputy sheriff for the county, and she was very much in love with my uncle. Unfortunately, she could never be Buzz's mate. Oh, he loved Nadine. He probably loved her as much as she loved him, but Buzz was a werecougar.

A Shifter. The only other nonhuman in town besides me.

Shifters only mated with other Shifters, with only a few exceptions, and all of those exceptions were paranormal mates. There was a distinct aroma that developed between mates, and when a Shifter caught the scent, it was for life. That couldn't happen in a Shifter-human relationship. It was genetically impossible. But since Buzz hadn't ever found his true mate, he and Nadine could be happy for many years together. Sadly, it would eventually end. And that was another reason to not get involved with sexy humans like Parker Knowles.

I felt an aching pain in my heart. My kind lived a very long time. Hundreds of years sometimes. I'm not sure anyone is built to watch the people they love grow old and die. I know I'm not.

"So Buzz is taking the big step, huh?" Parker smiled, his blue eyes lighting up with mischief. "He seems more like the rambling kind than the settling-down kind."

"Nadine has a way of getting what she wants." She reminded me a lot of Hazel. Nadine was very straightforward, a lot of "what you see is what you get." I admired her bluntness and her honesty.

I smiled at Parker; a melancholy feeling that I'd grown accustomed to experiencing washed over me. I knelt down, feeling the sudden need to hold on to something, in this case, my pittie. Smooshie put her wet nose to my ear and licked my cheek. I patted her.

"Theresa holding down the fort today?" I asked. She was Parker's other paid employee. He could only afford to have us both on part time thanks to an anonymous donation that rolled in every month on the fifth. Theresa Simmons, who had started as a volunteer, had worked at the Pit Bull Rescue Center for over two years. Parker also had several volunteers who spent time socializing the rescue dogs to get them ready for rehousing.

"Keith, Jerry, and Emily are in today, so she has plenty of help."

"Good, I hated leaving you short on a Saturday. I know that's when you run your errands, but it was the only time Mr. Peterson had open to meet with me."

"Life happens." He glanced over at me, his blue eyes locking on my gaze. "They don't get much better than Merl Peterson. He gave me my first job, did you know that?"

"No, you never told me."

"Yeah, he likes to hire local teenagers for odd jobs. He'd hire me occasionally for things like deck building and roofing. Summer work. It was long hours but a decent paycheck."

"My first job I clerked at a convenience store. I worked nights and some weekends." I'd had to quit school to work full-time, and the Valhalla Gas & Go was the only place that would hire an eighteen-year-old dropout.

"I'm glad you're putting down roots here." He looked around, his upper lip curled a little in disgust. "Even if it's this place."

"The house has good bones," I told him.

"That's not a house."

"It has doors and windows and rooms and—"

"Ghosts."

"Parker."

"Facts are facts, Lily." He walked up the front steps as if drawn, his voice like that of a tour guide. "Randall Dilley, who built the place back in 1908, hung himself in the living room. Another owner, Lincoln Edwards, was killed in a combine accident in the 1940s, a whole family disappeared from here in the eighties, and there hasn't been someone living there since Old Man Mills died in the upstairs bedroom two years ago."

"Let me guess." I mockingly gasped. "He was murdered."

"Nah. Natural causes." Parker paused. "Or so they say…" He let it hang there as if to imply there were more sinister reasons behind the old man's death. What he didn't realize is, because of my witch ancestor's gift, I could smell bull-poop from a mile away.

Anyway. I knew a little about John "Old Man" Mills. The property had been held in escrow as the court tried to find a blood relative somewhere to inherit. No one came forward, so the property was sold to Merl—who'd sold it to me.

"You want to go on the supply run with me?" Parker asked.

"No thanks." I smiled. "Another time. I want to get in and measure the rooms. I need to figure out where I want to start with this place. Besides, Buzz is bringing out the trailer today."

"That's fast." His lips thinned. "Well, thought I'd ask."

"And I appreciate it." To lighten the mood, I asked, "Do you think the ghosts took him out?"

"Who?"

"Old Man Mills, of course."

"I think he's one of the ghosts now." He moved in close, his tone ominous. "Some say when the moon is full, and the wind is right, you can smell his farts on the breeze."

I giggled. "That's terrible."

I will not flirt with Parker. I will not flirt with Parker. It had become my mantra. A mantra that failed fifty percent of the time.

I knew Parker liked me. A lot. I could scent his attraction. For whatever reason, his desire for me smelled like honey and mint. Crisp, refreshing, and exciting. But he deserved to be with a woman he could grow old with, and I had a terrible feeling that if I allowed myself to love Parker Knowles, I wouldn't be able to give him up when the time came for me to leave Moonrise. I could only stay for so long before people would start asking questions about why I didn't age, and the first rule of integrating with humans was to never let them know you were different. Not unless you wanted to be hunted down like an animal.

Humans had two impulses when it came to things they didn't understand. Kill it or dissect it. I didn't want either of those things happening to me.

Renee George

CHAPTER TWO

AFTER PARKER LEFT, I grabbed the toolbox, shovel, and scraper and took it into the house. The peeling blue ivy wallpaper in the living room gave the house the haunted feeling Parker had mentioned, but it was the most updated of all the rooms. It had drywall, not plaster, which meant, unless there was mold, I could save money by just stripping the wallpaper and painting in there.

Even with all its many failings, I already loved the place. I felt as if I'd finally found a home. A place to call my own.

I set the toolbox down. Getting started would be the tricky part, but I wasn't afraid to work hard. I would need to hire a contractor to tell me which walls were support walls, and which ones were room dividers. The place could literally tumble down around my ears if I decided to get sledgehammer happy.

Smooshie's ears perked. She stared at the door with expectation then began to bark the moment I heard the gravel spinning under the tires. I had great hearing, but Smooshie's hearing was incredible. I went outside. I grinned as I saw Buzz's blue pickup pulling his twelve-by-sixty-foot trailer onto my property. Behind him was a brown four-door car, its hazard lights blinking as they made slow progress up my drive.

When they got close, Buzz stopped, stuck his head out the window and shouted, "Where do you want it!"

I pointed to a piece of flat ground about twenty feet from the house. It was the side closest to the well and the power meter. I'd have to pay someone to come out and hook up the water, electric, and run a pipe to the septic tank, but I'd put money aside for that purpose already.

Five men — two in their forties or fifties, one that looked to be in his teens, and two who looked somewhere in between — got out of the brown car and began methodically getting down to the business of helping my uncle land the trailer.

They worked efficiently to get it blocked at the wheels, unhitched, and level.

Buzz got out of his truck and grinned. "It was a scary drive."

"I bet." The other men joined us. "Who're your friends?"

"Lily, these are some of my lodge brothers. This is Nick Newton." Buzz gestured to one of the older men. His hair was a dirty gray, which meant he'd probably been a light or dark blond before age changed the color. His hazel eyes were warm, and the deep leathery lines around his mouth and eyes marked him as someone who'd spent his life in the sun. "He owns Handy Contractors, and I've known him long enough to know he'll only rip you off a little." Buzz's grin matched Nick's.

Nick shook my hand. "As opposed to a lot," he added. I could smell tobacco on him, but his fingers weren't stained yellow, so I put him at under half a pack a day, maybe less. "This is Paul, Jeff, Mark, and my nephew, Addy." He cuffed the younger man behind the ear. "Addy's the Moonrise varsity quarterback. The kid has a great arm on him. Next year, if he can stay out of trouble, he'll have his pick of colleges if he can get the team to state." The older man beamed with pride at his nephew.

Addy was the youngest in the group. I'd seen him before at The Cat's Meow. He was usually surrounded by a couple of buddies, including James Hanley, a real jerk of a kid, and fawning over teenage girls. I'd heard the name Addy at their table, but I'd always assumed it was one of the girls.

"Addison," the teenager said, automatically answering my unasked question. His cheeks reddened. "It's a family name. I'm used to Addy, though."

I gave him a sympathetic smile. "It's nice to meet you, Addison."

The young man gave me a glance that was decidedly grown up, so I gave him one back that conveyed a when-hell-freezes-over message. He blushed again.

Paul was Paul Simmons. Late thirties, early forties, less gray than Nick and shorter, but well-built and handsome. He was a plumbing department manager at Hayes Home Improvement Center. I wondered if he was related to Jock Simmons, the lawyer Parker had used when he'd been suspected of murdering Katherine Kapersky. I hoped not. I didn't have much use for Jock. I believed he beat his wife, Theresa, the other woman who worked for Parker at the shelter. In my book, any man who puts his hands on a woman is despicable, but a man who hits a woman he vows to love is not only despicable, he's disgusting.

"I've heard nice things about you, Miss Mason," Paul said.

I wondered from who. Buzz wouldn't go out of his way to talk about me. He was a private person for obvious reasons.

I peered up at Paul. "It's all true."

They all chuckled at the small joke, and the introductions continued.

"Mark is the new guy," Buzz said.

Mark Stephens was the fourth guy. Mark, it turned out, was an electrician by trade.

"I've been back here for two years, and I graduated from Moonrise with Jeff here." Doesn't that count for anything?" He laughed and shook his head. "When do I get to stop being the new guy?"

"When another new guy joins the lodge," Nick teased.

"I was the old new guy," Buzz added.

The last fellow, Jeff Callahan, was Parker's age, it turned out. He and Mark had both graduated high school with Parker. Jeff had a beer gut that hung over his belt, which he sincerely needed since he had no butt to hold up his jeans. He was an accountant, which surprised me. I usually thought of pocket protectors and thick glasses when I thought of someone into numbers. This guy looked like a good ol' boy and smelled heavily of marijuana. My brother used to smoke it, so I was intimately familiar with the scent.

I smiled, though, when I realized Buzz had brought me a contractor, a plumber, an electrician, and... Well, I wasn't sure how Jeff's accounting skills would come in handy, but it felt like Buzz had stacked the deck in my favor.

"I can't thank you all enough for helping Buzz get the trailer parked and leveled. I wish I had a working kitchen, I'd invite you in for coffee or something."

"Buzz is paying us with a free meal tonight."

"It's my turn to bring dinner for poker night."

"Yep. No kids, no wives, no bosses," Jeff said, nudging Buzz. He looked at me. "No offense, ma'am." He raised his arms. I noticed he had a couple of rubber bands around his arm. It reminded me of my dad, who would take the rubber bands off the mail when he got it and put them around his wrists until he could move them into his desk drawer. Most of the time he forgot. My mom would snap him with them every time she passed him. I loved watching the two of them together.

"None taken. Now if I were your wife…" I raised my hands in a shrug. "Then I'd be sorry."

"Now that's the truth," Nick said.

"Hey," Jeff said defensively.

We all laughed. It was nice. It was a community. My community.

"Lily, Nick said he'd come out and inspect the house for you if you want. He can give you a good idea of what it's going to need."

"That's great. I really need to know what walls are load-bearing. I want to expand some of the spaces. I guess I'll have to deal with wire and plumbing as well."

Paul piped in, "Come by Hayes when you're ready. I'll give you a good deal on plumbing supplies."

"And maybe a little help installing?"

Paul grinned. "Maybe."

"Thank you." I beamed at Buzz. In the five months I'd lived in Moonrise, these humans had made me feel more welcome than I'd ever felt growing up in a town full of Shifters and witches.

"No problem. Hey," Nick added. "Tell Parker I really hope he can make it to the celebration Saturday night."

"There's a celebration."

"Coach Thompson," Addy said. "My football coach. He's retiring this year, and the school is having a banquet for him. They want the entire '09' state champion team to present him with a lifetime achievement award. Lots of folks coming into town for it."

The teenager didn't seem very enthused at the prospect of losing his coach. "It must be hard losing him right before your senior year," I said.

Addy looked up at me, his expression grim. Nick laughed though. "I've been that man's right hand for fifteen years. He's a great coach, but I have my own ideas of where to take the team next year."

So Nick would be the new coach. The kid forced a smile at his uncle, but it was easy to see he wasn't thrilled about having Nick as the new head coach.

"I'm sure it will be great," I said diplomatically, then changed the subject. "I really do appreciate you all coming out here today and for the offer of help."

When Buzz's friends finally crawled back into their car and left, he put his arm around my shoulders and turned us around to look at the house. "Home sweet home," he said. "I'm proud of you, Lily."

My parents were long gone now, but when Buzz said that to me, I heard my father's voice for the first time in eighteen years. It made my eyes water. "Thanks."

"You okay?"

"Yes. I'm just really glad to have found you."

"Me too." Buzz stared at the thick trees off in the distance. "That'll be a nice place to run," he said.

He was talking about a four-legged run, cougar-style. The lovely, large plot of land and the isolation of being surrounded by trees and wide-open farmland had been a big selling point, ghosts or no ghosts.

"Did you know John Mills? The guy who died here?" I asked him.

"Yes," Buzz answered. "I heard he got pretty senile there toward the end. Dementia took him hard."

Poor guy. He'd had no family to help him. "Parker says the place is haunted."

"Parker doesn't want you to leave his garage apartment." Buzz chuckled. "Ever."

"Don't you worry about what Parker wants."

Smooshie barked her agreement right before a squirrel in a tree caught her eye. She ran break-neck speed to the base, her barks, high and excited.

"At least the dog is happy," Buzz said.

"I'm happy, too." I crossed my heart. "Promise."

Buzz's expression grew somber and pinched. "You know it's not a sin for Shifters to have friends and lovers. You don't have to be alone. You just have to be realistic about your expectations."

"I'm not alone, and I'm not lonely," I lied. The thought of dating someone other than Parker had crossed my mind. The problem was, I only wanted to date Parker. I didn't want to bother with another man, human or Shifter.

Buzz had once been in love with my mother, it was before I was born, but she and my father had been true mates. It had been the reason Buzz had left our hometown and never returned. It's why I didn't doubt that he loved Nadine, but they would never have children. That only happened when a Shifter found his or her mate. Buzz and I had talked about how unfair it was to Nadine, but he assured me that she didn't want kids anyhow. Once on a girls' night out, she'd also told me she wasn't interested in having a baby. I could understand her position. I'd never wanted children of my own either, but that had been when my brother Danny was alive.

Did I want them now? Did Parker? I'd never be able to give him a son to play ball with, or a daughter to...well, he could play ball with her too. I smiled a little.

"Earth to Lily," Buzz said.

"I have plenty of friends around here, and I don't need a lover."

"Yeah. Right." He gestured toward my home. "Can you use some help with the house? I'm happy to help with some of the demolition."

I laughed. "Since I'm not dating, I'm going to use all my pent-up energy to give the walls a work over. I need to take the inside down to the bones and see what I'm working with."

"Asbestos, mold, and lead paint, if I had to guess."

I laughed again, and Buzz joined in. I loved the rich tone of his laughter. Again, he reminded me of Dad. "You're awful."

"Did you get the place inspected for mold and stuff?"

"Not yet. I plan to do it this week." I shook my head. "But even if I have to strip it down to nothing but studs, I'm going to return the charm to this old place."

"You really do like it, don't you?"

"Why are you surprised?"

"I bet Nadine you bought the place just so you could run away from Parker."

I looked around my isolated property. "I bought the place so I could run." I grinned.

Buzz and I drove out to the state park a couple of times a month to placate our other halves, but my cat was itching to get out more. I had no idea how Buzz managed not to go stir crazy in town with all the watchful eyes of the community on him. I guess he had a lot of years of practice. I shuddered at how many times I'd let my eyes change or a claw slip. Out here, there were no homes for miles, and my house had a long driveway. Add that to the woods covering the back half of my twelve acres and my Shifter hearing to warn me of anyone arriving, and I was in werecougar heaven.

"And I plan to run a lot."

"I get it," he said.

"You want to stay for a while? We can get a quick rabbit hunt in." And by hunt, I meant more of a chase and not catch. I preferred my food cooked on a stove to raw and possibly wormy.

"Tempting. But I have a thing tonight."

"Oh yeah, poker with your lodge buddies. Thanks for getting your friends to help with the trailer move. I'll call Nick tomorrow to have him come out and look at the place."

"Then you'll have to thank him. They volunteered when Merl and I told them what you were doing out here. I don't know Jeff or Paul well, but Nick's a good man."

"Merl Peterson?"

"Yes, he'd been with the Moosehead Lodge for thirty years."

"Do you all get naked and beat drums while you pass around a spirit stick?"

"Only on days that end in Y." Buzz leaned down and kissed my forehead. "I best get going."

After a brief goodbye, Buzz took off for town. I leaned up against my truck and watched the gray squirrel taunt Smooshie by leaping from branch to branch. She whined and clawed at the trunk. In a few minutes, she gave up and ran to me, her whole butt wagging as she pushed against my leg.

I reached down and petted her between the ears. "Okay, Smoosh, let's really have a look at this property." I took my clothes off—shoes and socks first, followed by shirt, pants, bra, and underwear. Smooshie cocked her head sideways, giving me a quizzical look. She always did that when I got undressed. It was as if she were asking, "How come your fur comes off and mine doesn't?"

"Don't worry, girl. The fur's about to really happen now." I dug her training clicker from my pants pocket and gave her the command to sit while I clicked it. Obediently, she sat, her tail swishing, creating a windshield wiper effect on the driveway gravel.

I knelt down in front of her, willing my cougar forward, exalting as fur rippled along my skin and every bone in my body transformed from human to giant cat. The entire process took seconds. I stared at Smooshie through my predator eyes. The first time I'd changed in front of her, she'd shied away, but she hadn't tried to attack. Now that she'd seen me go from Lily to cougar and back to Lily many times, she just got excited. Cougar equaled a run, and Smooshie loved to run.

I gazed over at the tree line behind the house. I touched my forehead to Smooshie's, the signal to go. She practically headbutted me as she jumped up on all fours. I laughed, but it came out as a throaty purring sound.

I detected the scent of decaying leaves where the ground had thawed, new grass, and a myriad of squirrels, raccoons, and deer scents. Smooshie ran like the devil chased her, hopping over fallen logs, ditches, and a small brook like she was a champion show pony. At one point, she face-planted with a yelp. I padded to where she'd fallen, but she was already up and running again.

There was a hole in the ground, a couple of feet deep. Something had dug up the dirt, but it was partially filled in, and grass was beginning to sprout along the upper edges. I leaned down and inhaled. Most likely a gopher had made the hole, but it was old enough now that I couldn't scent any one type of animal.

After some more exploration, I found there were many depressions in the ground in my woods. They had varying degrees of depth and flora growth, indicating that whatever species had dug these areas, had been doing it for years.

A rustle of sticks stole my attention. Smooshie was digging next to a mossy boulder. I guess she didn't like having holes on her land unless she'd created them herself.

I flushed with happiness. Smooshie could dig all she wanted out here and no one would get mad at her or me about it. Yay.

CHAPTER THREE

SOFT WHIMPERS FOLLOWED by labored pants woke me up. I peered out of one eye at the giant pink tongue hanging above my face. Smooshie needed a breath mint. A big one.

"What time is it?" I asked, without expecting an answer. I felt around my nightstand and found my phone. The screen was offensively bright. Five-seventeen a.m. Noooo. I had another hour and almost forty-five minutes before I had to get up for work.

I closed my eyes. "Dear, dear, Smoosh," I said. "You need to get your bladder on my schedule."

She put her front paws on my stomach.

Umph. "Fine. I'm awake." As soon as I moved her aside, she jumped down from the bed and wagged at me impatiently. "I'm moving," I told her and sat up.

I gazed around at the little apartment I'd called home for the past five months. This would be one of the last times I got out of this bed.

I stretched, and my back cracked like a bundle of firecrackers. I would not miss the fold-out couch bed. At all.

Smooshie barked to let me know I was going to be cleaning up a puddle if I didn't put some urgency into my "moving."

I wore a tank top and a pair of pajama pants to bed, so I just threw on a sweater and slipped on my galoshes. Parker's fenced-in backyard had been a bit marshy this week. I didn't bother brushing my teeth or combing my hair. Smooshie didn't look as if she'd last much longer.

She bowed to me at the door, stretching her own back as I clipped her leash on. "Soon," I told her, "I'll be able to just open the door and let you out when you have to go. The whole place will be your personal potty paradise."

I opened the door, and she dragged me down the steps to the gate between the garage and Parker's house. I could hear Parker and Elvis out back and wondered if that's why Smooshie had suddenly needed to pee at this unhealthy hour.

I tried to smooth down my frizzy bed hair, but I knew without a brush and some water, my actions were futile. When we rounded the corner, Parker tossed a ball toward the back fence, and Elvis took off after it. He saw Smooshie and me about the time Elvis returned with his prize.

Smooshie tugged hard toward them. She totally wanted in on the action. Parker grabbed another ball from his back porch. I unclipped my anxious pit bull, and she started running toward the back end of the property before Parker even lobbed the toy.

He laughed as he gave it a hard toss past her. "Morning. You're up early."

"True story," I said. Self-consciously, I tried smoothing my hair again.

Parker smiled. "You look fine."

"I know," I said a tad defensive. "I'm still waking up is all." I didn't want him to think I cared what he thought about my appearance. Even though I did care. "You're up early too."

"Elvis was restless." Parker threw Elvis' ball again then retrieved the other from Smoosh and threw it for her. "I think Elvis knows Smooshie's leaving."

I raised a brow. "And that's made him sad?"

"Well, he's gotten used to having her around." He shrugged. "Even if she's a little disruptive."

"Uh-huh." I was pretty sure it wasn't Elvis who felt restless.

"You want to come in for coffee? These two can stretch their legs for a few minutes without us."

"Sure." Oh, how I wished I'd have brushed my teeth!

Parker's kitchen smelled like freshly made toast and rich Columbian coffee. A medium-dark roast, which I knew was his favorite. He poured me a cup and set it down on the small circular table that filled the floor space. I took a seat in front of it.

"I can put you some bread in the toaster if you're hungry. Theresa brought some Irish butter over this week, and it's really good."

"Coffee's perfect." The Irish butter sounded tasty, but eating before I'd even had a chance to pee seemed somehow wrong. Parker sat across the table from me.

"I still can't believe you're moving out." He tapped is fingers on the table. "I was just getting used to having you around."

"You'll see me almost every day. It's not like I'm quitting my job here." I sipped the hot brew. Parker didn't respond, and the silence was deafening. I didn't want our friendship to be awkward. I wanted us to be easy with each other, but it had become a tug-of-war between my conflicting emotions for him. It wasn't Parker's fault. Other than the one time we almost kissed, he hadn't tried to put any pressure on me to be more than a friend, even though his scent and body language said he wanted more.

I filled the quiet between us with small talk. "You think we'll get another frost before the end of March?"

"Usually do," Parker said. "But it's been warming up fast. The thunderstorms will be rolling in soon."

"They get pretty bad around here?" It had rained a few times in February, but nothing terrible.

"Yeah, but not like the flatter areas of the state. We get the occasional tornado warning, but I've never seen anything come from it. The weatherman is calling for some severe storms this week." He shook his head. "In school, they would put us through these drills where we had to sit against the wall in the hallway and put our heads between our knees. We used to joke it was so we could kiss our ass goodbye."

I smiled. We had witches who urged harsh weather patterns to miss our town, so I'd never experienced what Parker was talking about. I wondered what my life would have been like growing up in a place like this, with its beautiful simplicity. "Speaking of school, I ran into a couple former classmates of yours, a Jeff Callahan and Mark Stephens."

Parker's expression changed to curious. "I played ball with Mark. I didn't realize he was back in town."

"He said he lived here in Moonrise. Two years now, apparently. Oh, and Nick Newton asked if you were going to be at some retirement party this weekend."

"Coach Thompson, my high school football coach. I'm still thinking about whether to go or not." His expression held a melancholy I hadn't noted before but he shook it off. "Mark's really back in town? Two years now? Wow. I had no idea. We lost touch after he moved. Jeff used to be a friend too. I haven't really talked to him in years either. Where did you meet them at?"

"They all came out and helped Buzz bring the trailer out to the new property. Him and Nick Newton, Mark Stephens, Paul Simmons, and Nick's nephew, Addison." Jeff didn't look athletic. At all. "Jeff played football?"

Parker grinned. "He rode the bench mostly, but he was part of the team. That's all that mattered." He shrugged. "Small town."

I liked that in Moonrise, even geeks could be jocks. Still, it surprised me. All of Buzz's lodge brothers had seemed like decent guys. I still wondered about Paul, though. "Is Paul Simmons related to Theresa's husband?"

"He and Jock are cousins, I think. Why?"

"No reason. Curious is all."

"I don't know him well." He sipped more from his cup, his blue eyes flashing on me briefly. "Jeff's an accountant."

"Yeah, I know."

"Apparently, he makes a killing during tax season." Parker sighed. "It seems like all my high school teammates are doing well for themselves."

Did Parker think because Jeff had a degree that it meant he was better somehow? I hoped not. Parker was the best man I knew. "If it makes you feel better, he's a total pot head," I blurted out.

Parker's eyes widened, and he scootched forward. "Seriously?"

"Totally." I grinned. "I could smell it when he stood by me."

"You know he's an instructor out at the college."

"He works at the college too?"

"According to his bio." Parker turned in his chair, opened a cabinet drawer, and pulled out a flyer and set it on the table.

"What's that?"

"It came with the invitation. It's the 2009 3A State Football Champions. The whole team is listed, along with their accomplishments."

I skimmed down until I landed on Parker's name. "Parker Knowles. After an honorable discharge from the Army, Parker settled back home in Moonrise, where he runs a rescue shelter for American Pit Bulls and Pit Bull Breeds. He is currently single."

"That's me in a nutshell," Parker said.

I scanned the brochure and saw a few names a recognized, including Jeff's and Mark's. Bridgette Jones' name was at the very end with two others, Michael Duffy and Travis Mount, on the "Deceased" list. My heart pinched. She'd been Parker's high school sweetheart, but she'd been nuts.

"Why are there female names on here? Did you all have girls on the team?" It seemed very progressive for the area.

Parker laughed. "No. The cheerleaders were invited as special guests as well. They supported us all the way to state."

"Go team," I muttered as I stared down at Bridgette's name. She had taken her own life after she'd tried to kill me and failed. I was surprised they'd included her. I figured the town of Moonrise would just as soon forget that they'd born a murderess into the world. Especially after it made the national news.

The press had made Parker out to be a local hero who took down a husband and wife murder team despite the incompetence of the county police. Yet another reason Sheriff Avery hated my guts. It hadn't happened that way, exactly, but I was more than okay with not landing in the spotlight.

I read a few other biographies, a nurse, a human resources manager, a pharmacist, a safety engineer, physical therapist, and the list went on. Parker's class only had thirty-nine students. I couldn't believe how many of them had gone on to complete college degrees.

"Oh, look." I pointed toward the end of the bio list. "Ryan's in here. He played too?" I didn't wait for Parker to answer. "Ryan Petry. Degree in Veterinarian Medicine from Missouri State University. Ryan has a successful practice in Moonrise, where he treats both domestic and farm animals. He teaches introduction to veterinarian medicine at Two Hills Community College. He is currently single."

"He's a catch," Parker muttered. He and Ryan were friends, but he was jealous of my friendship with the handsome vet.

I'd had lunch and a couple of dinners with Ryan over the past several months, but our relationship was not a romantic one. I'd told Parker before that Ryan and I weren't dating, but he didn't seem to believe me. If Parker had been a Shifter like me, he'd be able to scent my lack of attraction to Ryan. Hell, he'd be able to smell, like I could, Ryan's lack of attraction to me.

"Speaking of Two Hills Community College," I said, moving the conversation away from Ryan. "I think I might check it out."

"For classes? What are you planning to study?"

I wasn't exactly ashamed to tell Parker that I hadn't finished high school, or that I needed to take a GED class, but after seeing all the successful biographies of Parker's classmates, I felt self-conscious. So, I skipped the middle step to my goals and went straight for, "I've always wanted to study medicine."

"You want to be a nurse?"

I did not roll my eyes. I wanted to. But I didn't. "That would be an honorable profession, but no, I want to be a doctor." Or at least I had for the past twenty-seven years. Up until my eighth year, I'd wanted to be a pretty, pretty princess.

For the past couple of months, I'd been thinking about practicing a different kind of medicine, though. It was one of the many reasons I enjoyed Ryan's company. He'd even offered to hire me part time to work in his office and assist him out in the field on occasion. I wasn't sure how Parker would react, but I was seriously considering the job. Especially now that I had a home that needed a substantial investment for improvements.

Hazel had lent me the ten-thousand dollar down payment and enough scratch to get my utilities hooked up, but I would still have to come up with a five-hundred dollar mortgage payment every month, pay back my BFF, and find spare money to buy items to fix up the place. Buzz giving me his trailer to stay in was a huge weight off my mind. It meant I could make repairs on my own timetable. Years of poverty had taught me to be an amateur plumber, electrician, and carpenter. I had basic skills, but I knew at some point, I'd have to hire professionals.

"That's great, Lily," he said. "You'd be a really good doctor." He leaned forward and pushed his fingers across the table toward mine. Only inches separated us, and I could see a gentle longing in his expression. One I'm certain matched my own.

"I'm not sure if I'll do it or not," I told Parker. "I'll check out their programs and settle on something, though."

"Do you need some time off tomorrow to go out to Two Hills?"

"I'll go on my lunch break." I turned the handbill over. The back had candid shots of the 2009 Moonrise football teams, and their cheerleaders, of course. I recognized Parker in several group shots and one where he was standing next to a hulking guy who made him look like a dwarf.

"Who is that?"

Parker's face lit up. "Adam Davis. He was the class clown. Real nice guy off the field, but on the field, watch out." His eyes stared off into the distance. "Just another friend I lost touch with. You never think that's going to happen when you're in school. I really thought we'd all be hanging out forever. I left for basic two weeks after graduation." He tapped a picture of him, Mark, Jeff, Adam, Ryan, and some guy I didn't recognize. "When I got home two years ago, I felt like I was wearing the wrong skin. Sometimes I still feel that way."

He was singing my tune. Only it had been the opposite for me. The whole time I'd been in my hometown, I'd felt like an alien trapped on a hostile planet. Moving to Moonrise changed that for me.

I caught Parker staring at the guy in the picture I didn't know. "Who's that?"

"Mike Duffy."

I recognized his name from the deceased list. "He was a good friend?"

"The best. We'd been best friends since kindergarten. The six of us hung out all the time, but I was closest to Mike. I couldn't believe it when my dad told me he died. I was still in service at the time."

"What happened to him?"

"Some farm accident." His eyes crinkled with a brief wince of pain. He moved the conversation to his other friends. "Adam and Jeff hung out a lot. They were an odd pair, but they had a lot in common. They both liked numbers, for one thing." He smiled at the memory. "Adam had a good head on his shoulders. He got a concussion his first semester at college. It pretty much ended his football career. Really, he was the only one of us good enough to play at that level. He became an engineer instead."

"And Ryan and Mark?"

"Yeah, those two palled around. They were inseparable in high school. We all hung out, though. In school, they called us the 'Big Six.'" He smiled again. It made his face, which had seen too much death and war, appear young.

I looked down at his high school pictures again. I could see the boy in the photos when Parker smiled. The details for the weekend event were centered on the back. "The dinner honoring your coach and team is next Saturday. You need me to work extra here so you can go?"

Parker shrugged. "Maybe." He shook his head. "A classmate, Naomi Wells, has been calling me for the past week. She wants me to go with her to the Saturday night dinner." He looked at me as if gauging my reaction.

I pursed my lips, my mood souring. "Then it's settled. I'll stay here next Saturday night and hold down the fort while you enjoy reminiscing about the good old days with Naomi."

"You don't mind?" His voice was soft.

My throat tightened with emotion. "Of course not. Not at all." I stood up and looked out the kitchen window.

"Shoot! Smooshie is digging her way out under the fence."

"She's tenacious," Parker said, standing up and looking outside. Elvis, of course, was happily sitting and watching.

Impulsively, I grabbed the flyer and shoved it in my pocket when Parker stood up to look. "I'll see you in a little bit," I said and hurried out the door to stop my Hairy Houdini from making a grand escape.

CHAPTER FOUR

THE MORNING PASSED quickly, with a new intake, a black and white male named Dexter, brought in by Keith Porter. This was the second new one this week. The other, a gray female we named Star looked practically starved, and Keith said she'd been overbred to the point of malnourishment. Star was a sweetheart, and Ryan seemed certain she'd recover well.

When Dexter was walked past the kennels, the loud barking from all the dogs thundered up the hallway. It was a cacophony of sound that reverberated throughout the center.

Until I'd started working for Parker, I'd never heard anything like the noise these dogs could generate. The place smelled like dog, of course, but we tried to keep it clean, so there was always an undercurrent of lemon, pine, bleach, and Lysol. Blankets and towels were washed as needed, but we had a lot, so it didn't have to be every day. Unless the smell grew too pungent to handle. In January, the washing machine had broken down. We started throwing the soiled items outside because it got too bad in the utility room, and they'd frozen to the ground. It hadn't been our brightest move.

Keith Porter was a tall, lanky fellow, a little younger than Parker in age, and his brown hair and the scruff on his face always reminded me of Shaggy from Scooby-Doo. Theresa had confessed to me when I first got to town that she'd been having an affair with the young man. I didn't judge her. Her husband was a monster, and according to Theresa, he'd made several threats about what would happen if Theresa tried to leave him. When I asked her if he hit her, she didn't deny it.

Parker worked outside most the day with the dogs. He was also setting up a new run fence for the pit bulls who needed to be kept separate from the other dogs, even with supervision, until they could be properly socialized for rehousing.

It was Theresa's day off, so I cleaned all the three social rooms by myself as Parker and Keith took the dogs, one by one, out for exercise, training, and play. I put clean covers on the couches, picked up any poop, mopped up any pee, and swept the floors of dirt, debris, and dog hair — though pit bulls didn't shed much, thank heavens — and made sure each one of the kennels had food and water.

Smooshie, who followed me everywhere during my chores as long as the other dogs were kenneled or outside, had learned to leave the food and water alone. The afternoon volunteers usually cleaned the kennels, but if they were bad enough, I'd do it in the morning too. The dog beds were made of PVC and vinyl, so they were easy to wipe down, and the blankets were changed out when they got too smelly.

I threw myself into work to keep my mind off Parker and his event. Why had I said I'd cover for him so he could go with another woman? Was Naomi Wells tall? Beautiful? With a name like Naomi, she probably had the body of a supermodel. She'd been one of the team's cheerleaders, and I'd snuck a peek at her bio on the flyer. She was a journalist for the *St. Louis New Dispatch*, which meant she was smart.

Dang it! I wanted to be happy for Parker. We were friends. That's it. That's all I wanted. Just because I wasn't seeing anyone didn't mean it was fair for me to expect him to stay celibate and relationship-free too. On some level, I think I'd hoped he would.

No, I told myself. Be happy for Parker. He deserves to be loved. He deserves to be loved by someone who isn't lying to him all the time about who and what she is. Someone who can give him babies. Someone he can grow old with.

I walked down the hall after I put away the barrel of dog food in the supply closet, and was surprised to see Theresa, crying as she talked to Keith. Her blonde hair was curled and flawlessly set, and she wore a pale-green going-to-church dress suit that complimented her creamy peach skin tone. She was clenching a piece of paper in her hand.

"Theresa," I said as I came up on them. "Are you okay?"

She thrust the paper at me. "Someone knows, Lily."

I uncrumpled the note. I recognized the large capital letters immediately. The blood drained from my face. *I know your secret. Soon everyone will.*

This had to be the same person who had sent me similar notes when I'd first moved to town.

Anger bubbled inside me. "Where did you find the note?"

"It was under the windshield wiper on my car!" Her lower lip quivered. "What if Jock had seen it first?"

"Do you know it wasn't meant for Jock?" I asked.

"That's a good point," Keith said. "What if it was for Jock, not you?"

"Don't be stupid," Theresa snapped. "It was on *my* car, not his. Besides, Jock doesn't give a damn what people think about him." She walked over to the chair in the living room and slumped down into it. "Jock is going to kill me."

I tried not to get irritated with her for calling Keith stupid. Stress could turn even the best people ugly. "This could be some bored old bitty just trying to have fun with people." I'd read Agatha Christie's book *The Poisoned Pen* when I was younger. I hoped that's all these notes were. Nothing had come of the one I'd received in November. Two notes claiming to know my secret and nothing more. It had been long enough that I'd managed to put it out of my mind most days.

I put my hand on her shoulder. "You tell enough people that you know something about them, and you're bound to hit a few that will feel guilty enough to think it's a possibility."

"Oh, do you think so?" Theresa's eyes glimmered with hope.

"Definitely." I gave her a quick, supportive smile. "Now, don't let whoever it is see you sweat."

Keith gave me a grateful look as Theresa visibly relaxed and her tears dried up.

"I'm going to get lunch over at The Cat's Meow now that I'm done with my morning chores. Do you want to get a bite with me?"

"Thanks, but no, Lily. I have to get back home. Jock's parents are coming for dinner tonight, and I have a lot of food to prepare," she said.

"Another time then," I said.

Before I could leave, Parker came inside with a guy who was several inches taller than he was, and he had a big grin on his face. His eyes were lit with pure joy, and I couldn't stop watching.

He saw me and smiled wider. "Lily! I want you to meet someone."

The man, who was built like a lumberjack on steroids, leaned forward and held out a meaty hand. "Adam Davis," he said genially when I took his hand and shook. "Nice to meet you."

"You too, Adam." I looked at Parker. "I recognize you from the pictures of the football team. I'm sure Parker's glad to see you."

Adam gave Parker's shoulder a little punch. "This guy had an arm like a rocket, Lily. He could throw a ball like no one I'd seen."

"And this guy could block the defense in a way that normally took three guys."

"That's great." I had no idea what they were talking about. I never watched football. Ever. "It sounds like you two were superstars."

"Adam just got into town this morning." Parker sounded happy. "He's here for the Coach's retirement dinner."

"I figured so." I laughed. "Well, it's a good thing I'm free to work for you then. You'll have a great time catching up. I'm going to get some lunch. You want me to bring you anything back?"

"No, I got stuff in the fridge," Parker said. "I'll see you in a bit."

As I was leaving, I heard Adam say, "Please tell me you're tapping that."

To which Parker said, "Shut the hell up."

****

The Cat's Meow was packed with the local Sunday crowd. Buzz did great business on "the Lord's day." After all, who wanted to go home after sitting in church for two or more hours and then cook all afternoon? Besides, for some of the women in town, it was the only day of the week they put on dressy clothes and did their hair. I didn't blame them for wanting to take advantage of feeling pretty for a while longer.

Reverend Kapersky, who preached at Church of New Hope, rarely came into the diner to eat anymore. His wife Katherine, the woman killed by Bridgette Jones, had been a terror in the community, but the Rev was a good man. I was glad to see him sitting at the corner booth with Opal and Pearl, two elderly sisters who were practically fixtures in Buzz's diner. Opal had white hair, the color and texture of cotton, and Pearl, who was the more vain of the two, was always dying her hair a new color. This week it happened to be a pale lavender. I liked it.

I saw Addison Newton with a couple of girls and his delinquent friend, James Hanley. They were laughing and talking obnoxiously loud, and the tables around them were getting visibly annoyed. James reminded me so much of some of the boys my brother had started hanging around with. This was about the same time he started doing drugs and getting into trouble. I wanted to shake Addison and warn him that whatever he thought of himself, people would always think of him as his choices. Hanging out with a jerk like James Hanley was a choice.

Freda, Buzz's waitress, a tall woman with flaxen hair and a well-shaped body, especially for a human just past middle-age, carefully moved plates of food from a large tray down to a booth table just inside the door. It looked like all four patrons had ordered the diet plate—one large biscuit halved over crispy hash browns, smothered in sausage gravy, topped with thin slices of sharp cheddar cheese, two eggs, two slices of bacon, and two sausage patties.

Freda looked up at me and smiled. "Sit anywhere, hon," she said. It was her standard greeting when anyone entered the dinner.

I sat at the counter on an open stool and greeted the man sitting next to me on the left. He was drinking coffee and eating a gooey cinnamon roll. My stomach grumbled as I considered having both a diet special and a cinnamon roll for lunch.

Buzz peeked his head out the kitchen window. "Hey, Lily. I'm going to let you be my guinea pig for a special I'm planning next week. You game?"

"Breakfast or dinner food?"

"Breakfast."

Good. "Sure, as long as bacon is involved. Also, make my plate a double. I'm starved." I probably should have eaten before work this morning, but Parker's Naomi bomb had tied my stomach in knots. Shifters didn't skip meals, for good reason. Our metabolism was five times the rate of a human's, and we went into starvation mode if we didn't take in the calories of an Olympic swimmer in training.

"No worries," he said. He winked. "I think you're going to really like it."

Freda tapped the counter in front of me. "What can I get you to drink, sweetie?"

Most of the time I drank coffee, sometimes water, but on other occasions, like now, I wanted something sweet and cold. "I'll take a cola with a lemon wedge, lots of ice, please."

"You got it," she said brightly. She was always polite and friendly at the diner. She had been brought up in an era where customer service mattered. And for Freda, it meant great tips and job security. However, after I'd suspected her daughter Lacy might be a killer last year, she tended to ignore me if I saw her out in public. Maybe she ignored everyone when she was on her own time. I sometimes did when I'd worked as a waitress.

"Thanks, Freda." I felt a slight tug on my hair, not hard, just enough to get my attention.

"Hey, Lils," Nadine Booth said. "I thought I'd come have lunch with you."

Nadine worked at the sheriff's department, but she'd had Sunday and Wednesday off work this week, so she wore denim jeans and a dark-green sweater, instead of her tan uniform. She was tall, around five-eight, so I had to crane my neck back to meet her gaze.

"Hey," I said back.

Nadine sat on the stool to the right of me, and I swiveled to face her. "I thought you were getting Buzz's crap organized today."

"All his crap fit into a tiny trailer before making its way to my house. It took me all of about five minutes to get it organized." Her pale-green eyes sparkled with mischief as she said, "How hard is Parker pining, now that he knows your moving on?"

I tensed. "I am not moving on. I'm moving out."

"I'm just teasing you, babe." She stared over toward the kitchen window. I looked and saw Buzz humming as he happily cooked for a full house.

"Jeez, you got it bad," I told her.

She turned her eyes to me. "You're not lying, sister. That man makes my heart dance a foxtrot. I don't think I'll tire of looking at him." She grinned. "Or touching him. Or making sweet—"

I held up my hand. "I don't need you to paint me a picture. Just saying." Besides, I already knew more about my uncle's love life than any niece ought to.

"How's the new place? Do you think you can make it livable?"

"Eventually."

Freda put my cola down in front of me on the counter, and she slid a lemon-lime soda over to Nadine.

"Thanks," we both said.

"Hey, are you going to thing at the high school next weekend?" I asked Nadine. "I saw you were one of the cheerleaders."

"Only because they needed more girls. I let a friend talk me into joining that year. Still, I might go. I'm trying to trade shifts with Bobby Morris, my Monday for his Saturday, so it all depends on what he says. Why? You want to come?"

"No," I said a little too quickly. "Parker was talking about it is all." I shrugged. "He just mentioned a Naomi Wells."

Nadine's eyes widened. "Really? That's fascinating."

"Why?"

"Naomi was a real man-eater back in high school. She was the co-captain of the cheerleading squad and used to churn through boyfriends like a paddle in cream. She moved away after high school. Parker was talking about her? Do you think he's interested?"

"Maybe. No. I don't know. Naomi wants Parker to go to the dinner with her." I planted an elbow on the counter and my face against my palm. "He asked me if he should go."

"I hope you told him no, and not only no, but double-triple-no-no-no."

"I offered to watch the shelter for him."

Her expression was as disappointed as her tone. "Lils."

"He's a free man. He can date whoever he likes."

"I don't know why you don't lock him down, for the love of crackers. I've never seen him into anyone the way he moons over you."

"I can't." I took a long, sad, pathetic sip of my cola and belched. "Excuse me."

A hushed but intense conversation at a nearby table distracted me from my commiseration. I glanced back. Jeff Callahan sat at a table with a man I didn't know. It was the intensity that drew my interest. Nadine was still talking about Naomi Wells, going through the many, many broken hearts she'd left in her wake over her high school career, and how she'd moved away, yada, yada, but I was blocking her out so I could hear what was happening across the busy dinner.

"You owe me, Gary," Jeff said. "Who got you out of trouble when the IRS audited you two years ago?"

"Look, Peterson got the bid. I can't do nothing about that."

"And I can't do anything about an anonymous call to the government about some undeclared income."

"Now, Jeff," the man said. "I don't take kindly to blackmail."

"And I don't take kindly to liars."

"I never said I could make sure your auction bid was accepted. Merl's came in right at the end, and he offered more money. There was no way to *not* award him the land."

"Hey, Lily." Nadine poked my shoulder. "Where'd you go?"

I missed the end of the conversation as I turned my attention back to Nadine. "I'm here." I smiled at her.

"I thought you were having a seizure there for a minute."

Freda set a plate down in front of me. I stared down at the steaming special. It looked like a tall stack of blueberry pancakes surrounded by sausage links, with lots of butter and maple syrup over the top. There was a lot of food, but I was mildly disappointed. Until I cut into the stack and took a bite. My eyes widened, and I looked to the kitchen window to see Buzz grinning at me.

I swallowed the mouthful and cut into the pancakes again. "Bacon," I said, right before I stuffed my mouth with another large bite of fluffy pancakes with crispy, thick-sliced, Applewood-smoked bacon pieces cooked in. I hummed as I chewed.

"Good, right?" Buzz asked.

"Uh-huh," I grunted, already getting my fork loaded for the next mouthful.

"I don't know how you put food away like you do, Lily. You and Buzz have got the appetites of lions and the metabolisms of hummingbirds."

"Good genes," I muttered. I practically inhaled my lunch. In a few minutes, I was down to just the sausage links, and they were going fast as well. I really wanted to order a second plate, but Buzz had suggested I pig out at home and not in public, where the nice humans might freak out about me eating my weight in food.

"Oh. Em. Gee," Nadine said. She gaped in the direction of the entrance.

I looked up from my plate and glanced in that direction. A woman with long, silky golden-brown hair, a rosy flawless complexion, and a long, lean body walked in.

"Sit anywhere," Freda told her.

She wore designer jeans, calf-high suede boots, and a midnight-blue cashmere sweater. She was both beautiful and completely put together.

My stomach knotted. *Please don't be…*

"Naomi Wells," Nadine hissed in a whisper.

"Naomi Wells," I repeated. Had Parker seen her already? If so, I didn't have to worry about him liking me anymore.

She saw me, and her eyes flashed with something akin to recognition. Then she saw Nadine, and her mouth widened into a friendly smile. She strolled straight for us.

"Nadine," she said on approach. "It's so good to see you. You haven't changed one bit."

"I used to be twenty pounds heavier and had a face full of acne," Nadine muttered to me. To Naomi, she said, "Do we know each other?"

"It's Naomi." She pointed to her chest. "You remember, from high school."

"Oh, right," Nadine said. I could smell the sour lie pouring off her. "Naomi. Did we have gym together? High school is kind of a blur for me."

Naomi's eyes narrowed shrewdly. "Our entire class had P.E. together, and you were on the cheer squad briefly, but I can understand why you'd want to block those years out." She turned her gaze to me. "I don't believe we've met before."

"Lily," I told her. "I'm Lily Mason."

A hint of a smile tugged at the corner of her mouth. "It's so nice to meet you, Lily. Are you new to Moonrise?"

She wasn't lying, exactly, but the conversation felt fabricated. But why? "Yes. I've been here less than a year."

"How are you liking the place?"

"I like it just fine," I told her.

"That's lovely. I live in the city now, and I sometimes really miss Moonrise."

Nadine rolled her eyes. "I bet."

Naomi flashed Nadine a predatory smile then turned her attention back to me. "Pleasure to meet you, Lily."

Again, not exactly a lie, but this had been something more than a casual, accidental meeting. "You too," I said.

"I'll see you at the coach's dinner, Nadine," she said. "I guess I'd better find a place to sit."

"See you," Nadine said. When Naomi walked away, Nadine swiveled her stool to me. "You want to get a drink Wednesday night at Dally's Bar? I could really use a girls' night. Not too late, of course, but we could celebrate your new place with a couple of cold beers and maybe a shot or two." Nadine's eyes kept darting toward Naomi. "I can't believe I let her make me feel like I was in high school all over again."

"A girls' night out sounds great." I could use the distraction as well. There was something very slick about Naomi Wells, and I'd never trusted slick. "I better get back to work."

"Hey, if you need some help with your new place, let me know. Taking a hammer to something actually sounds awesome about now. Except Tuesday night. Buzz is taking me to that new Marvel movie, and I really don't want to miss it." She patted my arm. "But I would, if you needed me to help you with anything."

I laughed. "You enjoy your movie. I promise I won't need you."

Famous last words.

Renee George

CHAPTER FIVE

TWO DAYS HAD passed since the Naomi Wells bomb had been dropped on me. Other than to tell me he'd agreed to go with her to the event, Parker and I hadn't spoken much. I hadn't wanted to tell him that I'd met her, but she'd shown up at the shelter on Monday. She made a big thing about our "chance" meeting at The Cat's Meow. Parker gave her a tour of the shelter, and she offered to do a piece for the *New Dispatch* on the place to drum up more support. I disliked Naomi, but if her job could help Parker get more donations for the new shelter he was building outside of town, I'd put on my big girl panties and tolerate the woman.

I'd started on loosening the plaster in my new house. Luckily, the water and electricity had been set up for the trailer, and tonight, I would sleep on the property for the first time. It made me both sad and excited.

Sad, because there was no chance of running into Parker in the mornings before the rest of the crew arrived, and excited, because it was nice to have something that felt like it was all mine.

I swung a flat shovel nearly as tall as me against a wall underneath the staircase to the second floor. Plaster smashed to the floor in chunks. Smooshie skittered across the hardwood hallway and around the corner to the living room. She wanted no part of my foul mood.

Battery-operated lights illuminated the hall, living room, kitchen, and downstairs bathroom—not working currently, like everything else in this place—and with my Shifter vision, I could see incredibly well. I tapped the shovel along the wall to loosen the plaster from the laths, which were wooden slats that were attached in rows to the studs. It was the way they put up walls before the invention of drywall. And it was a pain in the butt. Real messy too. I wore a mask I'd gotten at the hardware store and a pair of safety goggles and work gloves. Every chunk of plaster that crashed to the floor filled me with satisfaction, and after the awful couple of days I'd had, I needed a lot of satisfaction.

Smooshie, who'd put several new holes in the yard and the woods the past couple of nights, began to race from the living room to the hallway and back. When a chunk would hit the ground, she'd slide to a halt and run away. It made me smile. Thank heavens for her. She was a real ally for me. No matter what else happened, she would never like Naomi better than me. That was some consolation.

I worked for the better part of two hours, stopping only for water breaks until the wall was nothing but a striped pattern of wooden laths. "I rock!" I shouted to Smooshie.

I heard her growling, not with menace, but more like when I played ball or tug-of-war with her. She was scratching against something as well. I took the mask and glasses off.

"What are you doing?" I asked, when I walked around the corner. She'd dug a section about the size of basketball out of the base of one of the only walls I wasn't going to have to tear down. The wallpaper and the drywall hadn't stood a chance. "Oh, Smooshie. Why?"

She had something in her mouth, and since I'd left the front door open to air out the place, she ran outside with her prize. I chased after her into the darkening night. She placed her possession into one of the holes in the yard and starting pulling dirt over it. More curious than worried, I walked to her spot. She plopped down on top of the hole as if to say, *move along, nothing to see here.*

"What you got there?"

She put her chin down on her feet, her eyes swiveling up to gaze at me.

"Let me see." I knelt beside her and put my hand under her belly. I felt something almost like papier-mâché once it dries. I gently gripped it and pulled it out from under the dog.

I could see pretty well in the dark, but still, I wasn't sure what the heck I had in my hand. "Come on, Smoosh. Let's go back to the house."

Once we were back inside, Smooshie jumped around my legs, hoping to get her hard-won prize back. When I got a good look, I nearly dropped the darn thing—because, holy Goddess in a pink tutu, I was holding a foot. I mean, it was brown and leathery, but I was pretty confident this was a human foot.

I examined it closer. The smell of decay was minimal. It had been dead long enough to lose the scent of rot. Also, it was missing a large toe. I hoped that happened before it was dragged out of the wall. I worried Smooshie had chewed it up like a rawhide toy.

"This can't be happening." I'd moved to Moonrise so I could stop being surprised by dead bodies.

Wait. There was no body. Not yet. Maybe this was the only thing. Maybe it hadn't even come out of the wall.

Smooshie was back at the hole, growling and tugging, and yanking on, dear Goddess, a leg with no foot.

"Smooshie! No!" I reprimanded. I dug the clicker out of my pocket and snapped it several times as I pulled her back. Was there really a body in my wall? The leather calf covered in a brown denim fabric sticking out of my wall pretty much meant yes. Yes, there were human remains in my new house. Ugh.

"You're destroying evidence, girl. Just sit and stay." She cocked her head sideways at me, the way she did when I got naked. I sighed. Just because Smooshie had found a body, didn't mean it had to be murder. Right?

Because people wall themselves up before dying of natural causes all the time, Lily. Don't be daft. I knew foul play was involved, but the idea of calling the sheriff's department to report another crime made my teeth ache.

Smooshie surged forward when I straightened. I clicked the trainer again. "Stay," I told her. Unfortunately, the foot she'd found already felt like a possession to her. Her massive chest vibrated with excitement as I placed the foot on the mantel over the fireplace.

Carefully, I pulled at the sheetrock, creating a big, wide circle of it around the area Smooshie had knocked out in her pursuit of a hidden treasure. The inside was stained brown with blood. I wondered if that's why wallpaper had been put up instead of paint. Had the blood soaked through the drywall? It took me less than fifteen minutes to expose the entire area, and less than five minutes to confirm that I was not unveiling a suicide.

The leathery corpse's dried-up, shriveled eyeballs stared right into the core of me, and the way the skin had pulled away from the teeth made it look like it was grimacing. It wasn't cold in the house, but I couldn't stop shivering. Smooshie's tail thumped on the floor excitedly.

"Stay put," I told her. She made a whining noise. My baby wanted desperately to play. "What in the world happened?" I asked the corpse. "Someone did a real number on you."

I'd seen worse things in my life, unfortunately. My brother's killer had made him virtually unrecognizable as a person. At least this victim was like a dried husk, not bloated and disfigured. Instead, the dark skin looked as if it had been shrink wrapped around the bones. The Midwest had high humidity and a fluctuation of temperatures. I'd read a mystery once in which it took almost a year of limited moisture exposure for a body to desiccate to this extreme.

I planned to call the sheriff's office, but Sheriff Avery hated me. He would find a way to make this body my fault. There was a hole in the side of the corpse's head and another in the chest on the right side. The one in his chest was jagged. Was it a knife? Or some kind of tool? I was assuming the one in his head was a bullet hole, but I didn't have enough experience with weapons to know for certain. The corpse's hair was thin, brittle, and choppy, as if the person had gotten a bad haircut right before death.

I allowed my cougar to surface. The world around me colored, and my sense of smell grew keener. I leaned forward and took a big whiff of the body. Must, mold, dust, hardly any rot or decay, even with my Shifter nose in action. It wore denim pants that were stained brown. The shirt was of the button-down western variety. It had decorations over the pockets and metal snaps. There were no shoes, but I imagined this was the kind of person who wore cowboy boots. The right side of his neck was more discolored than the other parts of his exposed skin. A tattoo maybe. It was hard to tell. I'd read that mummified skin could be rehydrated for fingerprints. I wondered if it worked the same for tattoos, or did the process damage the embedded ink?

I plucked a screwdriver, a flat head, from the toolbox and lifted the fold of the shirt. No bra. Which didn't really mean anything, but I decided this was probably once a man. Hadn't Parker mentioned a family disappearing from here back in the eighties? Was this the father? Was the rest of the family buried behind the other walls?

The idea was repugnant enough to make me pull back from the wall. I hadn't noticed that Smooshie had stopped thumping the floor with her tail.

My partial turn had her thinking we were going for a run. "Not this time, girl." I reached out, and she rolled her ear against my hand. I willed my cougar side to fade. "Such a good girl." Except for the finding-a-dead-body-in-my-home thing.

Her tail swished frantically, her mouth opened in her usual wide-mouthed, tongue-lolling grin. I scratched her behind the ear. "We'll run again soon, promise. Right now we have to deal with ol' Leather Face."

I turned back to the body. It was folded unnaturally. One hand was bent behind the corpse's back, the over was tucked into his side. He was making a fist. I reached down with the screwdriver again and gently pried at the clenched fingers.

A whispering crack made me stop. The tip of the index finger fell to the ground. Oops. I looked a Smoosh, who gave me an *Is that mine?* look. I shook my head. I stared down at the desecrated digit then back to Smoosh. "I won't tell about the big toe if you keep quiet about the finger."

She gave me a quick bark.

I grabbed my phone from my purse. When I turned it on, it beeped at me twice. Of course the battery was on the last leg.

"Okay, girl. To the truck," I told her, since I'd left my charger out there. "Come on." I did not need to have the phone die in the middle of reporting a body. That would not play well with Avery.

When I got Smooshie into the truck, I went around to the other side and climbed in. I started the engine and plugged my phone into the car charger. It made a couple of more beep sounds, then the lightning bolt indicating it was receiving external power showed up on the depleted battery image. Instead of calling the sheriff's department, I called Nadine.

I cussed myself for calling her on date night, but I'd panicked. "Hey, Chick," she said brightly. "We still on for drinks tomorrow night? You better not be cancelling on me."

"Hey, Nadine. Nothing like that. I...uhm..."

"Just spit it out, Lils. You need my help at the new place? My carpentry skills are terrible, but I'll happily take a sledgehammer to unwanted walls."

"Speaking of walls..." I proceeded to tell her all about Smooshie finding the mummy beneath some drywall, the two wound holes in his body, and what I could describe. I left out the part where I broke off his finger.

"Jesus, Lils. That's terrible. Which deputy took the call?"

"I didn't call the police."

Nadine made an eep-like sound, and we were disconnected.

I called her back.

In a very calm and official-sounding voice, she said, "Call the sheriff's office now, Lily. And don't you dare tell anyone you called me first."

"But you're coming, right?"

A brief pause made me fear she would hang up again. "Yes," she finally said. "I'll be there."

CHAPTER SIX

BEFORE THE FIRST responders arrived, Merl Peterson called. "Is it true?" he asked.

"I'm not sure what you mean?" Had I done something wrong?

"A friend of mine who works for dispatch called me. Did you really find a body in the house?"

"Oh. Yes. It was behind the living room wall."

He cussed a blue streak, apologized, then hung up abruptly.

Three hours later, I had two sheriff vehicles, one fancy white luxury car, and an ambulance lined up in front of my house. Deputy Bobby Morris, a tall man with dark skin and piercing brown eyes, was the first to arrive. He looked to be in his thirties, but it was hard for me to tell sometimes with humans, they aged at such crazily different rates. I'd seen women in their twenties who looked older than some in their forties.

It was the first time Morris and I had met, and I determined in a few short words that he had an honest countenance. He hadn't been friendly, exactly, but he'd been professionally courteous, and unlike Sheriff Avery, he didn't automatically dismiss me.

When the sheriff finally arrived, I'd been summarily kicked out of the "crime scene" and he proceeded to grill me like a steak burger at The Cat's Meow. The fact that he *smelled* like a steak burger added to the image, and frankly, made me hungry. I wondered if his wife knew he was topping off her health shakes with fatty red meat. A smile tugged at the corners of my mouth, and the sheriff stopped talking mid-sentence.

"Are you even listening to me, Ms. Mason?"

"I'm sorry, Sheriff." All his lecturing words had turned to blah, blah, blah. "What did you say?"

"I asked you if you touched or removed anything from the body or around the body."

"Uh, no." I thought guiltily of the screwdriver. "Other than the drywall, I didn't disturb evidence."

"And the foot?" He gave me a pointed look. "Why was it on the mantel of the fireplace and not in the wall?"

"Smooshie found the body, Sheriff Avery." I cast a glance at my truck, where Smooshie was poking her head out the opening at the top of the passenger window. She barked and whined, eager to join in on whatever fun she thought we were having. "She's a dog. They play with bones."

"And you let her?"

"I was in the other room. It wasn't like I'd planned to buy a house with a body in the wall."

"Uh-huh." He grunted as if he didn't believe me.

Nadine pulled in about that time with Buzz.

"Deputy Booth," Sheriff Avery said. "What are you doing out here?"

"Lily called me," she replied.

"After I called you all, of course," I said to the sheriff.

Nadine gave him a tight-lipped smile. "Buzz is Lily's only family. I thought she'd want some kin with her."

Buzz's red hair shined like copper wires in the spotlights Deputy Morris had set up. He shrugged when Avery glared at him before he looked over to me. "You all right, Lily?"

"I'm good. Thanks for coming."

"You got a nose for finding bodies," the sheriff said, interrupting the family reunion. "Why is that, Ms. Mason?" He eyed me suspiciously.

I asked myself that same question. Often. But to Avery, I said, "I didn't have anything to do with the

Kapersky murder, and I don't have anything to do with this poor guy's death. As old as that body looks, he was placed there long before I'd ever even heard of Moonrise."

His gaze narrowed on me as if he'd caught me in some big lie. "How do you know it's a he?"

"Oh, for the love of Pete," Buzz murmured.

"It's just a pronoun," I said. "I don't really know one way or the other."

"It's a man," a woman said. She had black hair swept up into a neat bun. She wore blue slacks and a silvery-gray silk blouse under an open windbreaker. She took off a pair of gloves and shoved them into her jacket pocket. "By the wear on his teeth, I'd put him mid-thirties, early forties when he died."

"Who are you?" I asked.

"Regina Crawford," she replied, offering me her hand. "I'm the coroner."

So she'd replaced Tom Jones. Interesting. Tom had been Bridgette's husband and accomplice to the previous murders in town. The coroner position was an elected one, which meant the coroner didn't actually need medical expertise. Tom had been a dentist. I wondered if Regina was a barber.

Not with that fancy car. "What do you do when you're not on county time?"

"I'm a GP at the family practice in town." She smiled. I could see amusement in her expression. "And what do you do when you're not finding bodies?"

"Ha ha," I said. Not amused. I guess I'd earned the remark though. "I'm glad the coroner has real medical knowledge. Are you state certified for medical examinations?"

She raised her brows. "No, not yet, but I'm working on it."

I heard a crackling over the police radio. Bobby Morris walked a fair distance from us and took the call. I could hear things like 1099 and 1053, and since I didn't know police code, I was clueless, but when I heard Bobby say, "Give me a minute," and shut himself into his vehicle, I figured it was something more than a traffic violation.

The sheriff walked over to his deputy's SUV and tapped on the window. The motor in the door squealed as the window rolled down.

"What's happening, Bobby?"

The deputy, who had been so calm and nonchalant when he'd arrived at my place, looked disturbed. "There's another body, Sheriff."

"Another mummy? What the he—"

"No, not an old body. A fresh one."

"Where?"

"Two Hills Community College."

"Who?"

Even quieter, Morris said, "Merl Peterson."

I felt the blood rush away from my fingers and feet. I glanced at Buzz. His face held a look of contemplation. He didn't show any of the alarm I was feeling.

"Get this scene wrapped up, Morris."

Without a glance back at me, Sheriff Avery jogged to his vehicle, got in and took off.

"What in the heck was that all about?" Nadine asked.

Buzz gave me a quick shake of his head.

I shrugged. "I don't know. Seemed urgent though. Maybe you could find out from Deputy Morris."

She brightened. "Good idea."

Regina Crawford's pocket beeped. She pulled out her phone. I craned a little her way and glanced at a text. It was one word. *Body*. It beeped again. *Two Hills Community College, behind admin building.* Regina said, "Gotta go."

I moved closer to Buzz when we were alone. "You heard all that, right?"

"Of course."

"Merl Peterson is dead. I talked to him tonight. He called right after I reported the body. Someone over at the dispatcher's office told him about it."

"You can tell the sheriff when Merl's death is public knowledge. For now, act like you don't know."

I could feel the tears doing their best to form. I took a deep breath. Was he dead because I found this old corpse. Was this somehow my fault?

As if reading my mind, Buzz said, "This isn't your fault, Lily. Or your problem. Let the police do their job."

I wondered if the sheriff would feel that way, about whether it was my fault or not. I was sure I'd be asked to provide an alibi. As to the "letting the police do their job," I was also sure the sheriff totally agreed.

Buzz put his hand on my shoulder. "Calm down. It'll be okay." He gave me a meaningful look. "Also, you have to stop reacting when you hear something no one else can. Okay?"

The conversation from thirty feet away had been crystal clear when I'd focused on the sheriff and Morris talking, it was hard to believe no one but Buzz and I had been privy to the conversation. Where we grew up, you just expected people would overhear you talking if you were in a public place. "I'll do better."

"I know. It just takes time."

Nadine came jogging back to them. She put her hands on her hips and shook her head. "You all are not going to believe this."

CHAPTER SEVEN

THE LIGHT PATTER of rain on the metal roof of the trailer woke me. Buzz had bought a memory foam mattress to replace his old one for me, and Smooshie was buried beneath the covers. A few times during the night, she'd awoken me with little barks and growls, her paws moving, as she dreamed of chasing squirrels. Or at least I hoped it was squirrels and not more dead bodies. My head hurt with the pressure that came with cooler weather, high humidity, rain, and lack of sleep.

It had taken four hours after I'd reported the body for the police and the forensics team to photograph, print, collect potential evidence, and clear the house. They'd cut out large squares in every piece of drywall to make sure there weren't any more remains buried in the walls. So much for saving money. The whole living room would have to be redone.

It was late when the last of the vehicles pulled out, and I was left alone. Buzz asked me to go back to his and Nadine's for the night, but I didn't see a reason for it. Surprisingly enough, I wasn't scared. Whoever had done that to the guy in the wall was probably long gone, and even if he or she wasn't, they wouldn't accomplish anything by scurrying out of the woodwork now. Even so, it wasn't until the rain started hours later that I finally fell asleep.

I shuddered now, praying my new home didn't have any more surprises. Like more corpses under the floorboards or worse. I stared at the ceiling, reluctant to get up. The bed was comfy, much more comfortable than Parker's pull-out sofa bed. I missed knowing Parker was next door, but I did not miss the apartment. I certainly didn't miss the sound of cars going up and down the road all hours of the day, and even some at night. It was peaceful here, if you didn't count the dead guy, and I needed peace. And distance.

The rain turned stormy, and the sound of it took on a thunderous beat. Smooshie wiggled herself closer to me and poked her nose out from under the blanket. She began to snore. I closed my eyes, wishing I had a good murder mystery handy. I still hadn't read the latest *Aurora Teagarden* novel by Charlaine Harris, but it was on my list to get as soon as possible. I really wanted more *Shakespeare* books, but I contented myself with the knowledge that Harris would keep writing stories, and I would keep reading them.

What would Aurora do with a dried corpse in her house? She'd most likely march down to the police station and snoop out crucial evidence that would put her on the killer's trail. If I went down to the police station to snoop, Sheriff Avery would probably have me arrested. I decided to stay away from the sheriff's office for now. Nadine would give me the scoop when she got it, but today was her day off, and she might not get any new information until tomorrow.

It was still a little dark out as rain sheeted down the windows and a brisk wind shook the trailer. My alarm hadn't gone off yet, so it had to be early. I wanted, make that needed, more sleep.

Something fell in the kitchen. Smooshie sat up at the same time I did. "Maybe it's the ghost of Old Man Mills," I said to her. I gave her my best spooky "OooooOOooooo."

Smooshie crooked an ear.

"A pan probably rattled out of a cabinet."

The dog stood up, stretching her front paws forward, her chin an inch from the surface of the bed and her butt high in the air. There was a reason the yoga pose was called "downward dog."

I looked at her. "Do you want to check it out or should I?" The trailer shook again as the wind gusted up. "We're not in Kansas, right?" Reluctantly, I got up and slid the door back to the small hall that led into the kitchen area. A cookie sheet was on its side, propped up against the bench seating that came with the pull-out table. "Yep, just a pan."

Lightning flashed, and the windows of the trailer lit up with the quick flash. Smooshie wedged herself under the table for shelter. "It's okay. Just a storm."

I didn't know who I was trying to convince more, her or me. I grabbed my phone from the counter to check the time. Dead. Crap on toast. I'd forgot to plug it in to fully charge when I settled in. I had no idea what time it was, and I couldn't check the weather or call for help even if I wanted to.

I plugged in the phone and started a pot of coffee. Was my corpse and Merl Peterson's death related? If so, how? Merl had only acquired the property recently. Whoever laid the drywall had to be responsible. John Mills had suffered from senile dementia, according to Parker. Someone could have put a body in the wall without him knowing, and even if he had witnessed it, would anyone have believed him? Would he even have remembered?

How could any of this have anything to do with Merl Peterson though? He was killed at the college. Wait, I take that back. All I knew for certain was that he was found dead at the college. Maybe he'd had a heart attack.

No, the sheriff wouldn't have raced off for an accidental death.

The way Avery had looked at me last night, I knew he thought I was bad luck. I wish I knew how Merl died. I also wished I knew who had been buried in my wall. Old Man Mills had died of old age.

Probably. No mystery in his death. There was the family that went missing in the eighties. Surely this wasn't one of them. Oh my Goddess. What if there really were bodies all over the place?

I poured a cup of coffee and sat down on the bench. Smooshie crawled under my legs. "Poor baby." I would have to remember to get her a Thunder Buddy vest. Parker and Ryan both swore by these kinds of dog jackets. They said it helped keep a dog from getting to anxious when they were scared or under stress. This was the first hard storm of the season, so I didn't realize she was so afraid. And the trailer amplified the noise.

Four hard bangs on the trailer door made my heart pound as I jerked upright in my seat. The storm had masked any car or truck noises. I went to the door and jumped again when three more bangs happened.

"Who is it?" I shouted.

"It's Parker!" he shouted back. "Let me in."

I undid the slide bolt, unlocked the door knob and opened the door. Standing in the rain, wearing a slicker and rubber boots, Parker looked like a drowning dog.

I moved aside. "Come in."

He dripped a huge puddle of water on my floor just inside the door. "Why didn't you answer your phone?"

"What?"

"Theresa told me someone was murdered out here. That you found the body. Why didn't you call me? You shouldn't be alone with another killer on the loose."

He looked so upset. I couldn't be mad at him for treating me like a victim, which I wasn't, because he had rescued me from Tom Jones. If Parker hadn't found me and hadn't stopped Tom, I would have bled to death. I had the bullet scar in my shoulder to remind me of my close call.

"I found a corpse, Parker, but it has been dead for a long time. There isn't any killer on the loose. At least not here."

"I thought...I heard Merl Peterson was murdered. It wasn't him?" He leaned back against the door, his eyes closed with relief. "I mean, an old dead body is bad, but..."

"I get it." And I did. Parker had been scared for me. "Merl Peterson was found at Two Hills."

"So he did die?" He wiped the rain off his face with a dishtowel I handed him. "I'll check in with my dad soon. He and Merl have been close friends for as long as I've been alive. Longer."

"Take off your rain coat," I said sympathetically. "I'll pour you a cup of coffee, and you can warm up while I tell you what I know."

I spent the next ten minutes relaying all the events from the night before. Parker chuckled when I told him about Smooshie trying to bury the foot in the yard. He gave her head a ruffling pet. I told him about Morris getting the call about Merl. I didn't tell Parker that I was over forty feet from him when he told the sheriff.

Once again I was reminded of why it would never work between us. The storm softened to a light patter again. "That's kind of nice," Parker said, referring to sound the rain created.

"It really is," I agreed. "Have you met the new coroner? Regina Crawford."

"Really? Doctor Crawford is the new coroner?"

So he did know her. "She seems competent. I think I like her."

"She works out of the same practice as my doctor. She just moved to Moonrise a couple of years ago. About the same time I came back home after my discharge."

"Nadine says she's going to the thing on Saturday," I said, kicking myself for the abrupt change of topic.

"Good," Parker said. "It'll be nice to see a friendly face."

"Naomi doesn't have a friendly face?" I hated that I was fishing.

Parker gave me a weary look. "Her face is fine."

I blinked. "Is it?"

He didn't elaborate.

"What time is it?" I asked.

He looked at his watch. "Eight-forty."

"Oh no. I was supposed to be to work forty minutes ago. I'm sorry, Parker. Go back home. I'm fine, as you can see. I'll get dressed and meet you there."

"You should take the day off. Theresa called."

"I know, to tell you about the body."

"No, she called to see how you were doing. When I told her you hadn't made it to work yet, she told me about the body. She was really worried about you."

As opposed to just wanting to gossip, he implied. "That's nice. I'll thank her tomorrow when she comes in."

"You can thank her on Friday. She came in to cover for me when I told her you hadn't arrived to work yet, so I gave her tomorrow off in exchange." He gave me a tight smile that said he'd been sick with worry.

"I'm all right, Parker. Honestly. I may have the name of a delicate flower, but I'm certainly not."

"I know that," he said. "Better than most. You're a strong woman, Lily Mason."

His use of both my first and last name made my belly flutter. Stop that, I scolded my mid-section. "Then you know I'm fine. I've been through lots worse than Moonrise has put me through, and I'll weather this as well."

"Why don't you ever talk about where you're from, Lily?"

My stomach clenched. "I talk about it." Lie. It was my fault the conversation had taken this turn, and I wished I could take back the implication about my past tragedies.

"Other than a few vague mentions of the friend who helped you with the down payment on this place, you never talk about it. Did you have a boyfriend there?"

"No." And I hadn't. I wasn't considered good stock for the Shifters, and the warlocks tended to like their partners with a lot more power or money. Which meant on this question, I was absolutely truthful with Parker. I just hoped he didn't ask questions I couldn't answer.

"Did someone you love die?"

"Yes."

"That explains it." He shook his head.

"Explains what?"

"You like me, don't you."

Oh Goddess, not this talk. Anything but this talk. "Yes." I gulped. "You're a good friend."

He shook his head. "When you lose someone, it can be hard to start over. It can feel like a betrayal. But the person you loved, who loved you, I don't believe he'd want you to be alone. To be lonely."

"I..." I put my hand on his. "I left home because my brother died. He was my responsibility, and I was a poor substitute for a real parent. He needed a mom and a dad but he got me instead." I fought the tears as I gave words to my deepest regret. "I came here because I have no one left for me back home. Buzz is my only family." I met Parker's gaze. "I'm heartbroken, but not for the reasons you think."

"So, you're not avoiding relationships, you're just avoiding a relationship with *me*."

"I'm not in a place to have a relationship with anyone." I gave his hand a squeeze. "Who did you lose?"

"How did you...? Her name was..." He paused, the word stuck in his throat. "Angela. Her name was Angela. God, I haven't said that name out loud in a long time. She was a radio operator for a unit my team was tasked with babysitting."

"And you loved her?" I felt a mild pang of jealousy. It made me feel like the worst kind of woman.

"I think so." He shrugged. "We knew each other for only a few months."

Sometimes that's all it took. "How did she die?"

He pulled the collar of his T-shirt away from his neck. "The firefight in Yemen happened. We were escorting trucks from her unit to an evacuation point. The truck she was in hit a land mine." He shook his head. "Angela didn't survive the blast."

When he'd told me the story before, he'd always said he "lost some buddies," as if he'd been distancing himself from the memories. He never used their names. Now I knew why. He blamed himself for Angela's death, the same way I blamed myself for Danny's.

"It's hard thinking about all the things you should have done different. Beating yourself up for this wrong choice or that bad decision."

His gaze met mine, and the whites of his eyes had reddened with unshed tears. "Copy that."

I was wide awake now, unfortunately for Smooshie, who'd already crawled out from under the table, went down the hall, and I heard the box spring make a noise as she put herself back to bed.

"I have some eggs in the fridge. Are you hungry?" I hadn't cooked yet in the small kitchen, so scrambled eggs would be a good test drive.

"Sure," Parker said. "Why not?"

"I have to warn you, Buzz got all the chef talent in our family. I know enough to keep myself from starving to death, but that's about it."

Parker laughed, and it was nice to hear after the weight of his confession. He stood up. "Why don't you let me cook? After all, I'm the one who barged into your place."

"You don't have to twist my arm," I said. "Pans are above the microwave."

He opened the fridge. "Wow, by 'some eggs,' you meant several dozen."

"I like eggs." They were quick and easy to make on top of being excellent protein sources for private pig-outs.

"And cheese," Parker added, pulling out a five-pound bag of shredded cheddar. "And dang, woman, you must spend half your paycheck at the butchers."

I forgot I'd stocked up on beef, pork, and chicken. I was going to divide it out when I had a chance and freeze some of it. "Cook," I said. "Don't judge."

He smiled. "Words to live by."

As Parker cooked, I remembered the argument in the diner. It probably had nothing to do with Merl's death, but the guy said Peterson, and I couldn't shake the feeling they'd been talking about

Merl. "Do you know a guy who works at the courthouse named Gary, or something like that?"

"What does he look like?"

"Middle aged, thin, glasses. I didn't get a long look at him." I hadn't wanted to be obvious I was listening. "Maybe his name was Greg. I think he works in the department where properties are auctioned."

"He doesn't sound familiar." Parker had found some bowls in a lower cabinet below the drain board. "Why?"

"It's probably nothing," I said. I didn't have any real idea the conversation between Jeff and the man had anything to do with Merl, so I didn't want to make a big deal out of it. "I hope Merl got all the paperwork filed on this property for me. If not I may have to jump through some hoops. Thought I could start with the guy in charge of that stuff."

"Contrary to popular belief, not everybody in a small town knows everybody else." He smiled when he said it. He cracked a dozen eggs into the bowl.

I smiled.

"I know you have a good appetite," he said. "My dad swears you have a tapeworm."

"Gross. I don't have worms." I drank some of my coffee. It had cooled a little more than I found pleasant, so I topped it with some fresh. "I'm part road runner," I said. "*Meep meep.*"

"That I believe." The stove's heating coil turned cherry red, and he set a frying pan down to heat. "Oil?"

"Counter." I pointed to where I had a canister of sugar, a canister of flour, and a quart of oil. What had started out as a potential disaster was turning into a nice moment between friends. I'd have to hold this memory, the one of Parker making me eggs, to get me through Saturday and Sunday. I wanted him to find someone to be with, I just didn't want to think about it, or imagine, or even better, I didn't want to know about it at all.

Was that too much to ask?

My phone rang. Parker leaned over to look at the display. "Sheriff's office," he said.

"Ugh. I do not want to face Sheriff Avery this early in the day."

"It might be important. Maybe they identified the body."

"Fine." I grabbed the phone on the third ring. "Hello?"

"This is Deputy Larimore from the county sheriff's department working in conjunction with the prosecutor's office. Am I speaking with a Ms. Lilian Mason?"

"Lily," I corrected. "Like the flower." They were my mother's favorite. "But yes, this is Lily Mason.

Can I help you, Deputy? Is this about the body found in my house?"

"No, ma'am. There was a body in your house? Did you report this?"

"Yes. Last night." Impatience colored my tone. "If you aren't calling about the body, then why are you calling me, Deputy Larimore?"

"I have been asked by the district attorney to inform you that a date has been set for Thomas Franklin Jones' trial, and a subpoena has been issued for your court appearance as a prime witness."

"Oh." Tom's attorney had managed to get two postponements already and I'd begun to think a trial might never happen. I was the main witness for the prosecution, since Bridgette had confessed her crime to me then shot me. Her husband Tom chased after me to finish what his wife had started. If it hadn't been for Parker, Tom probably would have killed me. "When?"

"May sixth, Ms. Mason."

"Thank you," I said. "Are you supposed to notify Parker Knowles?"

"I can't give out that information, ma'am."

"He's here with me now. I can hand the phone to him if you want, or I can just tell him."

"I'd appreciate you telling him," Deputy Larimore said. "Thank you, ma'am."

"What is it?" Parker asked as he stirred the eggs in the pan.

"Tom Jones." I suddenly had the intense urge to call for Smooshie so I could wrap myself around her for comfort. My own, of course. She was perfectly content to stay in bed. "They set his trial for May. Subpoenas are coming soon."

"That douchebag. He couldn't just go quietly away. I can't believe he recanted his testimony."

"He had enough money to afford an attorney who convinced him to fight." I sighed. I agreed with Parker. I wished every day Tom would vanish off the face of the earth.

"I don't know how he thinks he's going to go free. His wife killed Katherine. He covered it up. Then he killed Katherine's brother Ed, and he and his psycho wife tried to kill you."

I noticed Parker didn't say her name. He and Bridgette had been an item in high school. Prom King and Queen. They'd ruled the school, according to Nadine. And now, she was just Tom Jones' psycho wife. I touched my shoulder where Tom's bullet had pierced me.

"Does it still bother you?" Parker asked.

I put my hand to my side. "Not much." As a Shifter, I healed a little faster than humans, but without a healer witch's magic, the bullet's path had scarred enough to leave me with some stiffness. It had taken a lot of stretching and shoulder exercises to get most of the mobility back.

"This is such utter crap."

"I'm not looking forward to testifying." I shuddered at the thought of reliving the evening in front of a bunch of strangers. I'd have to work at controlling my emotions. It would be dangerous to let my claws come out mid-testimony.

Parker put a plate of scrambled eggs in front of me and opened three drawers until he found the utensils and handed me a fork. His expression was compassionate and sympathetic. "He's a coward."

"Most murderers are." I took a heaping bite of the eggs. They were good. Not too heavy with garlic, and just the right amount of salt and pepper. Smooshie jumped out of the bed, shaking the whole trailer with her acrobats. She scrambled into the kitchen, sat down, and looked up at Parker with those doughy, soulful eyes. She reminded me of a homeless waif straight out of a Dickens novel.

Parker laughed. He cracked an egg into the pan, mixed it up until it was just cooked, then tossed it in with Smooshie's dry dog food that I'd set up on the floor near the couch the night before. As she happily rooted around in her food, wagging her tail dangerously and making piggy noises, I knew she was falling in love Parker.

I looked up at him. He had his arms crossed over his wide chest, a smile on his face as he surveilled

Smooshie chomping away at her egg-laced kibble. He turned the wide charming smile on me, his blue eyes lit up with pleasure.

"Do you like your eggs?"

"Mmmhmm." I nodded and chewed and loaded up the fork for the next bite.

Yep. Smooshie was definitely falling for this guy.

CHAPTER EIGHT

DALLY'S TAVERN & GRILL was on State Street. It was half restaurant, half local dive bar, and filled with a combination of locals of all ages and college-age kids. It had taken me a couple of outings to get used to the chaos. Shifter bars tended to be quieter and less social, but really, outdoors was a Shifter's favorite place to drink. That way when the fighting broke out, there wasn't any property damage, and trust me when I say that if you have more than one Shifter drinking, there will be damage, be it someone's face or the nearest wall.

The wooden door with the rod iron handle that fronted the tavern had an old world feel to it that I liked. The interior was a combination of brick, metal, and neutral tones. The high ceiling was crossed with wooden beams with copper light fixtures dangling from them every couple of feet. Even so, the large room was dimly lit. The scents in the room were a combination of body odors, perfumes, colognes, hard liquors, and beer.

A pale blonde hostess, probably no more than twenty-one, met me when I walked inside. There were three people who trailed in right after me.

"How many?" she asked.

"I'm meeting a friend. Nadine Booth." I raised my hand and up over my head. "About yea-high, brunette, about my age." But really almost twenty years younger.

"Uhm, we've been pretty busy," the girl said. "Do you want to go in and look if she's here? If she's not, come back and I'll get you seated."

"Thanks." I smiled at her because she looked like a fragile thread ready to snap, and I didn't want to add to her stress. "I'll go look."

I heard her ask as I walked past, "How many?" to the folks behind me.

The bar side had two pool tables, two electronic dartboards, and one shuffleboard table, full-sized. I looked for Nadine. The seats around the bar were all occupied. I saw Ryan Petry sitting at a table with Ava Green, Lacy Evans, and Paul Simmons. Huh, I wondered if it was a double date.

Lacy was a single mom. The first time we met, she'd run a stoplight and crashed her car. She'd also left her baby at home alone because she'd only planned to be gone a few minutes. She was Freda's daughter, the one I had originally suspected of the Kapersky murder. Even though she hadn't turned out to be a killer, I still didn't like her very much. However, I liked Ryan a lot, and if she made him happy, who was I to disapprove their relationship?

Ryan looked up and saw me. He tipped his beer and smiled. I waved, and he waved me over. "Hi, Ryan," I said when I approached the table. "Night out, huh?"

Lacy and Ava gave me simultaneous *back off* looks. Paul Simmons stood up and shook my hand.

"Hi, Lily. Nice to see you again. You getting any work done on the house?"

How far out of the loop was this guy? "Not since the mummy."

"That was your place? Jesus Christ. I'd have considered moving to the moon if I found a body in my home."

"Our Lily's a cool cat," Ryan said. His word choice startled me for a moment, but I recovered when he winked. "You want to join us for some drinks?"

"Can't. I'm meeting Nadine." I scanned the room and found her. Finally. "There she is." I flashed Ryan a smile. "Talk to you later."

"You bet," he said.

"It was nice to see you again, Lily. Let me know if you need any help with the plumbing." Paul scooted back into the booth next to Ava. He looked over at Ryan and gave him a brief smile.

The reason it had taken me a second to find Nadine is that I had been looking for a woman sitting alone. When I landed on Nadine, she was sitting with the raven-haired coroner, Dr. Regina Crawford. Nadine saw me about the same time. Her wide smile blossomed as she waved me over.

"Hey, girl," she said. "Reggie here needed a girls' night out too." She gave me a meaningful look.

"I hope it's okay," Dr. Crawford said. "I don't want to impose."

"Of course not," I told her. "The more the merrier." But my mood soured. I'd wanted to ask Nadine some pointed questions about Merl Peterson's death, and having the doctor around was cramping my nosey style. On the other hand, Regina was the new coroner and might have some insight. "Where are you from, Dr. Crawford?" Her accent, like mine, wasn't Southern Missourian.

"I'm from Kansas City. The Missouri side, of course, and please, call me Reggie," she said. "I don't want to play doctor tonight."

"Unless some hot guy needs you to take his temperature," Nadine quipped.

Reggie and I flashed each other a look of surprise, then she started laughing and I joined in.

"He better be super-hot," Reggie said. Her black hair, which had been in a bun the previous night, was now loose and around her shoulders. It was shorter than I expected. Her dark brown eyes were warm, and I found myself really charmed by the city doctor.

I reached for small talk. "I can't believe the storms last night."

"They were bad," Reggie said. "The thunder shook my whole house several times. I thought I was in the middle of an earthquake for a moment."

Nadine gave her a look.

"What?"

She shrugged. "We're right on top of the New Madrid Fault."

"That's true," I agreed. "I read about it in a conservation magazine."

Nadine's eyes widened. "You're reading conservation magazines now?"

"Parker keeps them at the shelter. It's something to read during down time."

"And who is this Parker?" Reggie asked. She leaned forward. "Dish."

"He's my boss and my friend." Who just happened to show up at my place this morning and cook me eggs. "That's it."

"Is he attractive?"

Nadine giggled. "Yeah, Lily. Tell us. Is Parker attractive?"

I mouthed, *I hate you*, to her, but it only made her giggle more. "He's handsome, if you go in for his type."

Nadine wouldn't let it go. "And what type would that be?"

"I don't know." *Tall, rugged, muscular, beautiful blue eyes, smells good,* I listed off in my head. "You know, handsome."

"You paint a vivid picture, my friend." Nadine got up from her seat. "You want a beer or something stronger?"

"Beer's good to start."

"Back in two," Nadine said and headed to the bar.

"So," Reggie said, a sly smile turning up the corners of her mouth. "You want to know about the body you found in your wall?"

My lower jaw almost came unhinged. "Heck yes."

She rubbed her hands together excitedly. "Good. I've been dying to tell you since you got here."

"Should we wait on Nadine?"

"She already knows. Why do you think she asked me to come out tonight?"

I laughed. "I really like you Reggie."

"I'm easy to like," she said with a mild shrug then grinned. "So, the guy in your wall was a wanted felon."

"You're kidding me."

"I would not kid about this." She shook her head. "His name was James Wright, and he was wanted for bank robbery."

The guy had been dead for a while, so it couldn't have been a recent robbery. "How old was the case?"

"The robbery took place back in 1986." Her eyes widened for dramatic effect.

"The police have been looking for this guy for thirty years and he's been dead the whole time," I said incredulously. "How is that even possible?"

"But he hasn't," Reggie said.

"Hasn't what?"

"Been dead the whole time. When the medical examiner dated the clothing and bones, he determined the body had been dead around seven or eight years."

"So who put him in the wall and why?"

"Both excellent questions."

Nadine put a beer in front of me. "Did you tell her the best part yet?"

"I was getting there," Reggie said. She took a sip of her mojito. "That's really strong. Lots of gin."

"I think that's why this place is a favorite with the college crowd," Nadine said. "Now tell her or I am going to spill. I can't believe I didn't call you and blab earlier."

Reggie put her slender, well-manicured hand up. "Okay." She leaned in conspiratorially. "James Wright had a partner in the bank heist."

"And do the police think the partner killed Wright?" My heartbeat quickened. "Was the old man, John Mills, the partner? Oh man, how crazy would that be."

"Too crazy," Nadine said dryly. "John Mills was crotchety and grumpy, and a good farmer, but he was no bank robber. Would you let Reggie tell the story?"

"Fine." My heartbeat slowed. "He had a partner. Go on."

"Yes, he had a partner, a guy named Gail Martin. Gail was caught two weeks after the bank job just outside Poplar Bluff. That's about sixty miles from here. He was arrested, tried, and sentenced to forty years in maximum security."

"But they never found Wright."

"Nope, they never did. Until you dug him out of the wall yesterday."

"If his partner is in jail, then who would kill him? And why?"

Nadine piped, "I think his partner put a hit out on Wright for disappearing with the money and leaving him to face jail alone."

I raised my brow.

"It's a theory," she said a tad defensively.

"What about the wounds?" I asked Reggie. "Did the medical examiner find out what kind of blade made the chest hole?"

"A gun, actually. There was black powder stippling around the wound. The examiner said it was an extremely close shot. The gun was probably pressed against Wright's chest when it was fired."

"Maybe a struggle," I said. Thinking about how hard it would be to put a gun to someone's chest without getting disarmed. You didn't come at your prey from the front, not if you wanted the upper hand. "How big was the guy?"

"Six feet two inches. From the old photographs, he was pretty stocky as well."

I could see shooting him from across a safe distance, but who the hell had the balls to press the barrel to his chest without fearing for their own life? "Maybe it was an accident."

"Doubtful. The shot to the head was no accident, which is what killed him, by the way," Nadine said. "And neither was hiding the body."

"What about his hand? Did they find anything in it?" Other than a snapped-off finger.

"You're good, Lily. Yes. In his right hand he was holding something. It was really corroded, so the lab is doing some tests to see if they can get it recognizable."

"It was either something important to him personally, or a clue to the killer. You don't hold on to something that tight at the moment of death unless you think it has real value."

"Are you sure you weren't a cop in a past life?" Nadine asked.

"I'm just curious is all," I said. "There are too many rules to police work. Besides, I'd rather do what she does." I gestured to Reggie.

"Here, here." Reggie raised her glass and took another sip of her drink. I liked the way the mint and gin smelled together. I reminded me of Parker's mint and juniper shampoo.

Nadine's hand wrapped my wrist. I looked down at her fingers as she squeezed tightly. I met her gaze.

"Don't look," she whispered.

"What?" Automatically, I swiveled to look behind me.

Parker, wearing a black t-shirt, his best jeans, and a blue windbreaker, was being seated at a booth on the restaurant side of the tavern with Naomi Wells.

I shrank into my shoulders as the predator in me fought to climb out. My fingers curled under my palms into tight fists to hide my claws.

"I told you not to look," Nadine said.

"What is it?" Reggie asked. "Or who?"

"It's no one," I said tersely.

"Dang, girl, your voice just went all Hannibal Lecter." Nadine eased up on her grip.

I closed my eyes and took a deep breath to get my body under control. "I'm fine. Parker and I are friends. He can date whoever he wants."

"Oh, *the* Parker," Reggie said. "Where?"

"Left corner booth past the divider," Nadine said helpfully.

Only Parker's head was visible now that he had been seated.

"Okay, Lily," Reggie admonished. "You definitely left out some details in your description. That man is fine."

"He's all right," I grumbled. Stupid men.

"Who is the woman with him?"

Nadine answered. "That's Naomi Wells. Small-town-girl-makes-good-in-the-big-city story. She's a journalist in St. Louis, just back for a hometown celebration."

"I think I've seen this movie," Reggie said. "It was a *Lifetime Original*."

"Did everyone die at the end?" I wanted the disaster of a night over and done with.

"Lily!" Nadine said with surprise. She was smiling, though, so it hadn't taken her aback. "You're jealous."

"Am not."

"What do you think, Doc?" my Moonrise soon-to-be ex-BFF asked. "What's the diagnosis?"

"Chronic heartbreak aggravated by a severe case of jealousy. I prescribe marching over there and telling him to kick the city girl to the curb."

"Stop it."

Nadine touched my arm again. "I get it, Lils," she said more seriously. "You're scared to let yourself be with Parker, you're scared of getting hurt, but if you don't make a move, you are going to lose any chance of being with a guy you're crazy for."

I liked it better when we were talking about the dead body. "I think I'm going to call it a night. Smooshie is going to need let out soon. As it is, I fully expect the trailer to be trashed by the time I get home." I'd barely finished half my beer, but I'd lost my taste for it.

"Don't go, Lily," Nadine pleaded.

"I didn't mean to chase you away with my teasing," Reggie added. "You should stay."

"If you stay," Nadine said, "I'll tell you about Merl Peterson."

My ears perked. Shoot. Curiosity was this cat's Achilles' heel! I crossed my arms and leaned back. "Fine. Tell me about Merl Peterson."

"Merl died of blunt force trauma to the back of the head."

"Did he fall and hit his head?"

"Not unless he fell on a marble ball from "Floating Truth" an art display out back of the admin building and the ball crawled away after."

"Huh?"

"The marble ball, about the size of a grapefruit, was picked up and used to kill Merl. It was found about five feet from his body with blood on it."

"Someone bashed his head in?"

"Yes."

"Are there any suspects?"

"Merl's wallet was missing, along with his Mason ring. The sheriff suspects a robbery gone bad."

"Any prints on the ball?"

"No," Reggie said, getting in on the discussion. "It had Mr. Peterson's blood on it, but no prints."

"So the killer was smart enough to wear gloves. But the campus has classes at night, so it's possible this was just a crime of opportunity. Maybe the killer would have pounced an anyone walking in the back courtyard on campus." I had liked Merl. I didn't want to think about someone hating him enough to kill him on purpose. "What was Merl doing out there, anyhow? Do you know?"

Nadine shrugged. "No clue. You don't have to check in on campus. He could have been there visiting a faculty member or a student, or maybe he just liked to walk out there. Who knows?"

Merl knew. And now he was one more ghost to add to the Mills house curse. Now that I owned the property, was I next? I shook my head. I had an advantage. No one except Buzz knew I was a Shifter. And humans were a lot more fragile than my kind.

"What is it, Lils? You think of something?"

I shook my head again. "I'm just being silly. Parker told me about a curse on the Mills house. How all the owners have died or disappeared. Merl was an owner briefly, and now he's dead."

Nadine's brows narrowed together. "You think you're next? Don't be daft, Lily. John Mills lived in that house for eight years and died of old age. He was eight-nine when he passed on. That house didn't kill him. A long life did."

"You're right," I said. "I told you it was silly."

"Are you hungry?" Reggie asked.

My stomach growled at the mention of food. "Starving," I said.

Nadine laughed. "That's my girl."

Renee George

CHAPTER NINE

TWO ORDERS OF HOT wings, a platter of nachos, and a pile of cheesy bacon fries later, I still hadn't gotten over Parker being at Dally's with Naomi. I hadn't told him I was coming here tonight, but I *had* told him I was having a girls' night with Nadine. Had he purposefully brought her here to make me jealous? Gah! I was being ridiculous.

"Nadine Booth," a booming voice shouted. We all looked up. Parker's friend Adam strolled right up to our table.

"Jesus," Nadine whispered as she slouched in her seat. I hated to tell her, but hiding behind me would be an impossible feat.

He looked at me. "Nice to see you again, Lily."

I smiled. "Nice to see you too, Adam."

He grinned, his shoulders relaxing so you could see his neck. He really was a big guy. He craned his head sideways to look past me. "Nadine. It is you," he said. "I thought it was. Woo-wee, you have filled out nicely."

"Thanks. And you're still filled with hot air," she said.

"Aw, now, don't be like that." He smiled. "I'm only in town until Monday. Give me a spin on the dance floor for old times' sake."

"One dance," she said. "Then you go on. This is a girls' night, and the last time I checked, you were no girl."

"I'll let you check again if you want to be sure."

Nadine hooted with laughter. "I'll take your word for it."

As they went out on the small dance floor, I got a call from nature. I might have hollow legs when it came to food, but the second beer was putting serious pressure on my bladder. "I'll be right back," I said to Reggie. "Nature calls."

I passed the dance floor on the way to the bathrooms. Two couples aside from Nadine and Adam were slow dancing to a sad country song. Since I didn't keep up with music, I wasn't familiar enough to recognize it though. There was something about beer, bars, women, and apple pie. I pushed out all the noise from my head as I went into the nearest stall, dropped my pants, and peed, thankful for the semi-peaceful moment. My senses were so overloaded, I felt a bit fried. After, I went to the sink and washed my hands with hot water, then turned on the cold and splashed my face.

In the mirror, I saw that my hair, the color of dark cinnamon, had gotten wild since I'd left the trailer. The humidity this far south had given me a serious case of the frizzies. My skin had freckled a little more since the weather had warmed, and I spent more time outside. I wore very little makeup because most of the time I'd rub it without thinking. I once gave myself two black eyes at a high school party back home. I'd forgotten that I was wearing mascara and my eyes had been irritating me, so I kept scrubbing them with my palms. It wasn't until my friend Hazel pulled me aside and handed me a wet towelette and a compact mirror that I knew why a couple of high school jerks had asked me if I was related to raccoons.

I didn't wear mascara anymore. I usually didn't care that my eyelashes were almost nonexistent, but Naomi Wells had lush eyelashes. Which meant, tonight I cared.

The door opened, and my nightmare walked in. "Oh, hi, Lily. Fancy meeting you here." She laughed. It was loud and bawdy. I'd expected her laugh to be as pretty as she was, and I felt like a petulant child that her terrible laugh made me feel better.

"Hello," I said as I pulled some paper towels from the dispenser. She didn't make a move toward a stall like I expected. Instead, she moved in next to me, rummaged in her purse for some strawberry-tinted lip gloss and dabbed it on her full lips.

"You out on a date tonight?" she asked.

I had a gut full of nachos and wings and beer, and it made me surly. Still, I tried to be polite. "No, just out with some friends."

"That's right," she said. "You and Nadine, right?"

I remembered she'd been in the diner when Nadine had asked me to come out for drinks on Wednesday. Had she brought Parker here on purpose? And for what reason? It wasn't like I was competition. She couldn't possibly know I was even remotely interested.

"I better get back out there."

"Hold up," Naomi said. "I heard about what went down with Bridgette last year. I'm really sorry you had to go through that."

Numbness crept over me. Had Parker told her about that night? I'd never asked him not to tell anyone, but I felt betrayed all the same. "It was awful."

"Did Bridgette say why she killed Katherine?" Her tone was gentle but probing. It reminded me of Hazel when she was interrogating someone. Friendly, but insistent.

"I don't want to talk about it, Naomi. Sorry." Though why I was apologizing was beyond me.

"No, no," she crooned. "I'm sorry. It's just that...Bridgette had been a friend in school. It's hard to process how someone like her, so put together, could have done such an awful thing. It's a lot to take in. I was hoping you might tell me something that would make it make sense."

Bridgette Jones had been selfish and vain. She killed Katherine because she didn't want the older woman telling the town that her husband Tom was the father of Lacy Evans' baby, and then *he'd* gone on to kill Katherine's brother because Bridgette was worried Ed knew the secret as well. Both of them had tried to kill *me*. And now, because Tom recanted his confession, I would have relive that night over again. There was no way in the world I was going to do it here in Dally's bathroom with a woman I barely knew.

"There is no making sense of what Bridgette did," I finally said. "None. I'm sorry she was your friend, but she was responsible for two deaths, and she almost killed me. I wouldn't even know where to start explaining that kind of behavior."

"I understand," Naomi said. She reached in her purse again, and I heard the faint sound of an electronic beep. It wasn't loud enough for human ears, but just enough that I picked it up.

Play it cool, I reminded myself. *She's human. I'm supposed to be human. What she can't hear, I'm not supposed to hear.* It was probably nothing. She might have brushed against a button on her phone when she put the lip gloss away.

I didn't say goodbye as I walked out the door, but before I got three feet away, I heard my own voice say, "I wouldn't even know where to start explaining that kind of behavior."

It stopped me in my tracks about half-way down the hall, my nails sharpening into claws. Had she recorded me? I mean, of course she had. I'd just heard my words echoing off the bathroom walls. I hadn't said anything exciting or revealing, but that wasn't the point. Naomi Wells had followed me to Dally's, tracked me into the bathroom, and then recorded our conversation. What the heck was she playing at?

I walked away, my mood soured by the encounter.

Ryan Petry put his arms around me and swung me around before setting me down on the dance floor.

He smiled like a man full of bliss, his eyes shining like he'd used them to capture stars. He moved with me, his right hand on my shoulder to lead me, his left in my right hand. Luckily, I'd learned a few two-stepping moves from Nadine and kept up without tripping over my own feet.

"Lily, you look beautiful tonight." He grinned down at me. I could smell a mixture of blended whiskey, grenadine, and orange juice. My friend had been doing watermelon shots. They were a favorite of his.

"You're drunk," I said, glad to think about something other than Naomi and Parker.

"Yes, I am," he said. Then he lifted his lead hand from my shoulder and put a finger to his lips. "Shhhh. It's a secret."

I laughed. "Not a very good one. I saw some pictures of you in high school."

"Really?"

"On the back of that flyer. You were standing between Mark Stephens and Mike Duffy. Gosh, you all looked so young."

For a moment, his eyes grew sad. I had to bring up Mike Duffy, a friend of his who'd died, and totally kill his good time.

"I'm sorry, Ryan. I didn't mean to dredge up painful memories."

"What do you mean?" he asked in a way that said he really wanted to know.

"Your friend Mike died. I'm sure it was hard on all of you when it happened. Parker said he was away in the Army when his dad told him."

"Parker and Mike were like brothers. We all were. At least we were back then."

"What do you think about Adam? He's awfully loud."

Ryan laughed. "He's always been the life of the party."

"And Naomi?"

"Lily." Ryan gave a look of understanding and disappointment as he pulled me close. "She'll never shine as bright as you in Parker's eyes." He leaned back a little to meet my gaze. "Do you think I'm handsome?" He didn't smell like desire or lust, and he wasn't looking at me the way a man looked at a woman he wanted to bed, which meant, the question wasn't so much about what I thought. I realized Ryan was feeling insecure. But why?

"Are you okay?"

"I'm fine," he said. "Right as rain. Oh!" His eyes lit up. "Proctor's cow is about to calve in the next week, do you want to tag along?"

"You sure know how to show a girl a good time."

"Girls aren't the problem." He lost his smile for a moment, and then it returned. "Shhh," he said again. "That's a secret too."

I giggled as he twirled me under his arm and back, and when he pulled me in tight, I glanced over to where Parker's booth was on the other side of the tavern.

Parker stared at me, his eyes flickering away as I caught him watching. He looked miserable. Naomi sat across from him.

I looked up into Ryan's beautiful face, and said, "You are very handsome."

He dipped his head and kissed my nose. "Thanks, Lily. You always make me feel better."

"I thought that was beer's job."

He chuckled. "Sometimes beer needs a little help." The song ended and he let me go. "So, do you want a call when the calf comes?"

"Yes," I said. "That'd be cool."

"Great. I'll call you then."

I smiled. "Sounds good."

When I finally made it back to the table, both Reggie and Nadine looked at me expectantly.

"He's just a friend," I said with mild exasperation.

Reggie pursed her lips. "I'm beginning to think you say that about all the men in your life."

"Only when it's true." I tapped the table, cussing myself for the claw marks I'd left earlier. Thankfully, neither of my friends seemed to notice. "Okay. I'm going to call it a night. Smooshie is good at holding her water, but I'm pushing the limit."

Reggie smiled at me. "I hope we can do this again," she said. "I haven't had this much fun since the divorce."

I wondered if that's why she'd moved to the other side of the state from Kansas City, but I'd save that question for next time. "I look forward to it," I said. "I'm really glad Nadine invited you to join us."

I gave both women a brief hug and headed to the exit. When I got to the hostess area near the front door, Parker was standing there.

"Hey, Lily," he said. The way he stared at me quickened my breathing.

"Hey, Parker."

"I didn't know you'd be here tonight."

"Your date did," I said.

"Really?" His lost boy expression changed to one of disbelief. "How could she?"

"It doesn't matter. I'm glad to see you getting out. You deserve to have some fun."

"I'm not having fun," he said.

Good! "I'm sorry to hear that." It didn't seem hardly fair that people couldn't lie to me, even if they didn't always tell the whole truth, while I could lie at will. "I'm just on my way home. I need to let Smoosh out."

"I didn't realize you and Ryan were so close." His ears had reddened, but he seemed more hurt than angry.

It occurred to me that if Parker believed I was seeing Ryan, he'd stop trying to find ways to date me. But I couldn't bring myself to create that kind of deception, especially after I told him that I wasn't in a place to have any relationships. "It was just a dance, Parker. I'm really tired, and I want to go home."

"You mean to the trailer."

"Yes, that's exactly what I mean."

I moved past him and out the front door with unnatural quickness, knowing that Buzz would be more than disappointed if he knew I used my other half to avoid a petty human confrontation. I didn't care. I was at the point where it hurt more to be where I was, than I cared whether someone noticed something weird about me.

I'd parked two blocks down in a large car lot since there hadn't been any street space available when I'd arrived. It was only nine at night, so the streets were fairly empty except for a few people exiting other restaurants and bars on the street. I saw a couple who looked almost freshly out of high school, kissing up against a wall. I scowled as I passed them. Stupid young love.

When I got to Martha, I put my key into her rusty door. I felt restless with anger and raw energy. Smooshie and I were running tonight. We would run until our furry legs couldn't move.

I heard a slight click before a loud bang rang out. I reflexively ducked even as I told myself the sound was only a car backfiring. Goddess, help me. My shoulder scar ached at the thought of getting shot again. I'd never felt that kind of physical pain before.

Still shaking, but annoyed with my wussy response, I stood up. "You're being paranoid, Lily," I said.

That's when I noticed the hole in the framing around the door. I put my finger in it. It was still warm.

"Oh. Oh, crap." I grappled my phone from my purse and ran up the street toward the tavern.

Parker was outside with Naomi. When he saw me, I must have looked completely freaked out. "What's wrong?" He grabbed me by the shoulders, forcing me to look at him. "Lily, what's happened?"

"I was... Somebody..." I shook my head, fighting against my own denials. "Someone shot at me, Parker. They shot at me."

CHAPTER TEN

ONCE AGAIN, I found myself in my third least favorite place in the world. The sheriff's office. The second least favorite was the hospital. And my first least favorite was the morgue. I didn't need to end up there to know I wouldn't like it.

Sheriff Avery had made a point of coming in from home to interview me himself. His office was large with oak paneling that gave it a den vibe. He had a metal shelving unit filled with manuals. His desk was cluttered with files and scattered paperwork. On his desk was a picture of his wife, Margaret, and a picture of Theresa Simmons and her husband Jock. Theresa was Sheriff Avery's daughter. I wondered if he knew what a complete turd his daughter had married. Avery didn't strike me as the kind of guy who would let someone abuse his daughter. However, he did strike me as the kind of guy who was so wrapped up in his job that he wouldn't notice if something awful was going on in his personal life.

He thinned his lips. "Tell me what happened again."

I sighed. "I put the keys in my car door. I heard a gunshot. I ducked. When I didn't hear another, I stood up. There was a bullet hole in my truck."

"Do you think it was deliberate?"

"Maybe."

"Why would someone want to kill you, Ms. Mason?"

"I don't know that someone would, Sheriff Avery. It could have been a random shooting for all I know. Whoever it was didn't stick around to find out if their shot hit me or not."

"Could it have been a warning?"

"I don't know."

"Why would someone want to warn you?"

The more stupid questions he asked, the angrier I got. "I. Don't. Know."

My stomach burbled. And the sheriff raised his brows.

"Nachos," I said.

He grunted.

"Can I go home now?" Several hours had passed since my truck had been shot, and Smooshie was going on six hours without a break. "I have a dog who doesn't care why I'm late, she only cares that I'm late."

Parker had offered to go let Smooshie out, but I told him I'd call Buzz to do it. Which is what I'd planned, until Sheriff Avery hijacked my witness statement and turned it into an interrogation.

"Fine. You can go for now, Ms. Mason, but keep yourself available."

I winced and gave a quick shake of my head. "Where do you think I'm going to go, Sheriff?"

"Goodbye, Ms. Mason."

****

Other than one pile of poop and a pee puddle, Smooshie had managed to resist the urge to destroy the trailer. As a matter of fact, she barely picked her head up from the bed when I found her burrowed under the blankets in the bedroom.

I cleaned up the mess, changed into bed clothes, and crawled under the covers with her. "You're not in trouble, sweet girl. Tonight was my fault, not yours."

The covers moved as her tail swished. She licked my cheek and softly whined as my body began to shake. I'd been shot at. Again. At least I hadn't been hurt this time, but it didn't change the fact that it had brought a flood of past trauma up in me. I thought Moonrise would be different for me, but it seemed that no matter whether I was back home in Paradise

Falls, or here in this town, trouble seemed to follow me. It may have been why I entertained the idea that the house might really be cursed. I sometimes felt like I'd been born to bad luck.

I didn't realize I was crying until Smooshie crawled closer and curled her body into me. I wrapped my arms around her and just let go. My phone beeped. I ignored it. It beeped again. And again. By the ninth text message, I got up and grabbed the stupid thing with the thought of throwing it against the wall.

One message was from Buzz. One from Nadine. The rest from Parker. All three wanted to know if I was okay. Since I wasn't, I ignored each of them, put my phone on silent, and crawled back into bed. I tossed and turned. Not even the memory foam could take the tension from my muscles. I really needed to run.

I let my cougar slip into my eyes and flashed Smooshie a look I knew she could see, even in the dark. "Want to run?"

She scrambled from the bed, yanking the covers with her as she hit the floor and ran toward the front door.

"I guess that's a yes."

CHAPTER ELEVEN

THE NIGHT AIR was crisp as Smooshie and I explored the woods. There was a giant oak that was hollow near the base that completely monopolized the dog's attention, much to the chagrin of the squirrel family living inside the tree. I signaled her with a chuff, which sounded more like I was coughing up a hairball. She barked a couple of times, but backed off.

It was natural for her to want to hunt. I understood the compulsion to chase something down because their running away excited you. It happened to me every time I shifted, but I didn't want Smooshie to get comfortable killing small animals. It might start as a rabbit or a squirrel, but her aggression could escalate to other small animals, like dogs and cats. I'd heard it about my own kind my entire life, that once you got a taste for blood, it was hard to give up. Smooshie didn't have the same kind of reasoning to reel her back from the edge if she crossed the line from play to predator, so I preferred she just stayed ignorant to the bliss of catching prey.

I found more depressions in the ground. They seemed even more noticeable in the moonlight, because they looked almost like shadows where the light passed over the holes. I'd thought an animal had made them initially, a gopher or a mole, but they seemed uniformly spaced out.

I ran at the nearest tall tree and leaped up, grasping the bark with my front and back claws, digging in as I scaled the trunk to the lower branches. Smooshie excitedly tried to follow me. She managed to get a few feet and slid back. She tried a couple more times, than sat on her haunches with her neck craned back as she stared at me. A few high-pitched noises escaped her throat. That was her way of telling me that she wanted to play, but not this game.

I tried to reassure her, but while my cougar form could make plenty of threatening noises, there were only a couple of sounds I could make that might calm her, and I hated purring like a domestic cat. It just made me feel...precious. Blech. Instead, I used the sound to mean stop. The high, sharp, breathy cry dropped her to her stomach.

I examined the surrounding area, and tried to detect as many of the anomalies as possible.

A balloon of anxiety formed in my gut as I realized what I was looking at.

I jumped down from the tree, landing, of course, on all fours. It was a myth that cats always landed on their feet, but we managed to do it most of the time. I smiled at that, and Smooshie gave me a weary look. I must have flashed too much fang. I purred now, and she pushed her body against mine.

I sauntered to one of the areas I'd seen when I was up in the tree, and Smooshie followed. This was a mound, not a depression, which meant it had been filled in. Animals didn't usually dig holes then cover them back up. I sniffed around, detecting the faint whiff of something not quite right. Some grass was starting to grow in the dirt, which meant it had probably been dug up after the first thaw at the end of February.

I pawed at the dirt. Smooshie got in on the action, and she managed to move a lot of earth in a short amount of time. I roared, which sounded more like a baby's scream. Smooshie stopped digging. I inhaled deeply. It was faint, but I definitely smelled tobacco. I pushed the dirt around some more and found a crumpled brown cigarette butt.

It confirmed one thing to me: even if a lot of these holes had been made by gophers, some of them were created by a man or woman. Someone who smoked. I dug some more, but there wasn't any other human clues. It could have been dropped casually. Old man Mills maybe, hanging out in his woods. Squirrel hunting or watching while he had a cigarette.

Smooshie pushed against me. I pushed back and rubbed my cheek against her face. She rewarded me with a quick swipe of her wet tongue across my nose.

Ick.

I gave her a gentle head butt, my *let's go* gesture. I stretched my legs and took off in a quick lope. In a few seconds, Smooshie had caught up to me. I didn't run full speed, because while dogs are fast, cougars are faster, and I didn't want to leave my girl behind. The breeze on my fur made me feel freer than I'd felt since leaving home. It wasn't that I missed Paradise Falls. I didn't. But I missed being able to shift when I wanted and not worrying about whether someone would catch me.

As we raced from the back of the woods toward the trailer, I pulled up short as I heard a vehicle crunching down the gravel road.

Crap. Crap. Crap. Why did people keep showing up unannounced? Just because I didn't answer my phone didn't mean I was dead. Sheesh. And why couldn't I get a moment's peace on my own property in the middle of the night?

I'd never make it to the trailer before my uninvited guest. I pulled up short, but Smooshie kept running, and without my human voice, I couldn't tell her to stop.

I ran back to the tree line and hid. The truck was Parker's. I should have just messaged him back. If I had, he wouldn't have made the trip out here.

"What are you doing out here, Smoosh?" he asked. He leaned over and scratched her ear. "How's your momma doing?"

Inside, I smiled. Outwardly, more purring. Ungh. I hadn't thought of myself as Smooshie's mom, maybe a big sister, but definitely not a mom. It was kind of sweet when Parker said it though. I watched him walk to the trailer. He disappeared around the side of the trailer for a moment then reappeared with Smooshie on his heels at the front door.

I watched him hesitate with his hand in the air, knuckles forward, as he debated on knocking. Finally, he rapped on the door twice. "Lily?"

When I didn't answer because hel-lo, cat here, he knocked again. "Lily, you in there?"

He jiggled the door. It wasn't locked, which surprised Parker. I could see it on his face. I could also see the tightness in the way he moved that made me think he was afraid. I wanted to run to him and tell him I was okay, but...cougar.

Smooshie pushed past him and jumped up into the trailer. He followed her inside. A few seconds later, he came out and went to the house. I heard him yelling my name inside the place for a few minutes. After, he walked outside, his eyes squinting as he scanned the trees. "Lily!" He walked toward the woods. "Lily! Are you out here?"

Goddess help me. Why wouldn't he just give up and go home?

Because he was scared for me. I'd been shot at tonight, and now my dog was running around free without me, and I was nowhere to be found. Of course he was freaking out.

He pulled his phone from his pocket. "Yes," he said. "I'd like to report a missing person."

No, no, no. He called the police. I did the only thing I could think of to salvage the situation, I willed myself back into human form and shouted, "I'm here! Parker! I'm here and I'm fine."

"Uhm..." he pulled his phone away from his ear, "...hold on."

"I'm here!" I yelled again from behind a wide oak. My woods were full of them. "It's me, Lily. I'm okay."

"Never mind," he said into his phone. "False alarm." He hung up and shoved the phone back into his pocket. "What are you doing out here?" he yelled in my direction.

When I made no effort to come out of the woods, he started walking toward me.

"Stop," I said when he was close enough to hear me without shouting.

"Are you okay?" His eyes narrowed in my direction. His eyes were probably adjusted to the dark as well as a human's could, but it still didn't match my ability.

"I'm fine." I poked my head out from behind the trunk. "Why are you here?"

His expression changed quickly, as if I'd slapped him. "You didn't answer my texts and wouldn't pick up the phone when I called. I was worried about you."

"As you can see, I'm okay."

"I can see your head, but nothing about you hanging out in the woods in the middle of the night is okay."

"And why not? They *are* my woods. I'm not allowed to take a run at night?"

"Lily, come out from behind the tree." He took another step toward me.

"Parker Knowles, stop right where you are," I demanded.

He stopped again. "Lily, why won't you come out of the woods?"

Oh for Goddess' sake. "For the same reason you won't leave." The cool air was freezing my naked tushy. "I'm stubborn."

"You don't sound hurt." He took another step.

"I'm warning you, Parker. Stay back."

"What are you hiding? You got a body out here?" He was teasing now, but there was a mild hint of anxiety to his questions.

"The only body I'm hiding is mine."

"What?" His brows raised in genuine surprise.

Renee George

"I'm naked."

His breath left him in a hiss. When he processed my words, he said, "You're kidding."

I stuck a bare arm out then pulled it in. Next, I stuck a bare leg out. "Do you need any more proof? Because there might be a three-quarter moon in the sky, but behind this tree, it's a full-moon situation."

Parker started chuckling and quickly it turned into a complete belly laugh. Smooshie had walked behind me and tried to goose me with her cold nose.

"Stop it," I said, unable to temper the sharpness in my tone. Smooshie trotted back over to Parker, who was starting to wheeze. "Ha ha. Laugh it up. I really thought I'd have some privacy out here."

He finally got himself under control after a few minutes. Criminy, he'd been holding stuff in. Hysterical laughter was a stress-release mechanism. I'd suffered a few episodes myself over the years.

"This is not funny."

He chuckled again, but it didn't get out of hand this time. "It's really not. Who goes jogging in the nude?"

"Someone who has enough property to keep it private."

"Would you like me to bring you some clothes?" He shoved his hands in his pockets. "Or you just want me to go home?"

Part of me wanted him to go home. The logical part. But my other parts, the stupid parts, said, "Go get me some clothes. My robe is hanging on the back of the bedroom door."

He smiled, and it made me smile. Dang it!

We made a careful dance of him not looking while I put on the robe after he'd retrieved it from the trailer. He made coffee once we came indoors, and I sat at the table and let him. Smooshie, of course, crawled back up on the bed.

"Lazy," I said.

"What?" Parker asked. He set two cups down on the table. He'd poured both cups three-quarters of the way full.

"The dog. She's a lazy beast." I said it fondly. "She loves the memory foam."

"I bet it cushions all her bones just right," Parker said.

In my cougar form, I found that hard surfaces could make sore spots on my hips and shoulders. I understood why Smooshie preferred the bed to the floor, or even the thin cushions of the couch.

The aroma of the rich, dark roast made me sigh. I took a sip, and after standing naked outside, I was glad for the heat.

"This is good," I said. "Thanks, Parker. You make a heck of a good cup of coffee."

"The Army taught me more than just how to shoot guns," he said.

I met his gaze, and his eyes held warmth. He was kidding with me, which was good. Most of the time when he mentioned the Army, I could scent the stress on him. Not that I needed to be a Shifter to know when he was stressed, his body language usually said it all.

I smiled at him, but I couldn't force it up to my eyes. "We have to stop meeting like this." Tonight was a prime example of why. Parker showing up unannounced while I was in Shifter form could be dangerous for not only me, but Buzz as well. I thought I could be less careful out here, but not if I didn't make things clear with Parker.

"Someone shot at you tonight, Lily."

"I know. I was there. I heard the noise. Saw the hole in my truck." I stood up and went to the sink, a panic of epic proportions welling up inside me.

Parker got up and stood next to me. He turned on the cold faucet. "It's normal to feel freaked out. He wet his hand and wiped the tears I didn't realize were falling down my cheeks. The water felt cool against my skin. Parker's calloused fingers were more gentle and less rough than I thought they'd feel.

I took a deep breath, trying to find my center.

"The first time I was in a firefight, we were taking down a compound out in the middle of nowhere. There was nothing like your tree to hide behind. Not in the desert. We'd gone in at night. I stayed just far enough outside the perimeter of the target to stay out of sight, as the more experienced members of the team went inside to retrieve documents. When they came out, it was my job to paint the building for a drone strike and lay down suppression fire for the team if they came under attack on exit. I was calm and cool that night. Three Taliban ran out behind the team, shooting their weapons and raising the alarm. I fired my assault rifle in three-round bursts, and as soon as the team cleared the strike zone, we signaled for the drone strike. It was over in thirty minutes."

"Why are you telling me this, Parker?" I turned to face him.

He stroked a wild strand of hair away from my face. My body shivered.

"You feel feverish."

"I'm okay."

"I thought that too. I thought I was okay. I'd even felt a little elated. I know that sounds sick, but I did. I'd had guns shooting at me, and I'd been shooting back, and it had excited me in the moment." He shook his head, his blue eyes like shiny pools I could drown in. "The next mission, I was tasked once again to stick with the radio operator, while he painted the target and I covered the team's escape."

"And?"

"And I did my job. I didn't falter. But with the second victory, I didn't feel the same excitement. I felt sick. I…"

"Felt like you would explode from the inside out with all the anxiety you were feeling?"

"Yes," he said on a breathy sigh. "You know I suffer from PTSD."

I was aware of his post-traumatic stress. I was also aware of how close his body was to mine, and how good he smelled. I loved the scent of his shampoo and body wash.

"It didn't start with my injuries, or at least not the injuries that took me out of the Army. It started with the first mission, and every single one of them after that. That's how it works on you, even when you're brave." He smiled down at me. "And you're maybe one of the bravest people I've met."

I didn't feel brave, but Parker's comment pleased me. He always seemed to know the right thing to say to make me feel safe.

I wanted him to know me. I wanted it more than anything else in the world.

"I found my parents murdered when I was seventeen years old," I confessed. There was so little about my past that I could share. How could he understand that I was closer to his dad's age than I was to his age? I had more years of stories than he'd been alive. "I walked in to find them slaughtered in our home. I'd been out with a friend. My brother, Danny, he'd been home when it happened, but my parents had hidden him away. He saw them like that..."

"Like what?"

"Throats cut. Hearts..."

I let go of what I was about to say. There would be too many questions if he knew their hearts had been ripped from their chests. No human had the strength to pull off that kind of crime. It had been a combination of Shifter power and witch magic. Two things I could not discuss with Parker.

He didn't press me. "Oh, Lily," he said softly. "You really have lost so much."

His sympathy made me cry again. I thought I'd put those tears behind me, but grief could sneak up on you. It was like herpes, once you'd been exposed, it never really went away, and you never knew when it would rear its ugly head.

"I'm okay."

"You keep saying that, but I don't think you are. You were shot five months ago, and then someone shot at you tonight. There are bound to be emotional repercussions."

"Bound to be, huh?"

"Sorry, too many months of therapy. But it doesn't mean I'm wrong."

Renee George

He wasn't. I *had* been freaked out. The shot, whether accidental or deliberate, had shaken me up. Once you've had a bullet punch through you, you never wanted that to happen again. Ever.

"Now do you understand why I wanted to check up on you?"

"I get it, but I'm a big girl. I can take care of myself." I looked away as his stare become more intense. "I've been taking care of myself for a very long time."

He looped his finger under my chin and raised my face so that I would look at him. "I wish you'd let *me* take care of you, Lily. If only for a little while."

His voice was soft and low and it made my heart full. I hated myself for feeling both vulnerable and safe with Parker. I had secrets though. Secrets I could never tell him. "I can't," I said, trying hard not to sound as sad as I felt.

He put his arms around me and hugged me. "Yes, you can."

I stood there for a few seconds with my hands at my sides, my head against his chest, and his strong, steady heart beat in my ear, weakening my resolve. It felt good to be held. Until this very moment, no one had held me like this, comforting, loving, since my parents died. I put my arms around Parker's waist and pressed my palms against his back. We stayed like that for a few minutes, neither of us talking, other than the occasional, "It's okay," from Parker when I would start crying.

By the time we disengaged from holding each other, his blue T-shirt had dark spots where my tears and snot had landed. I grabbed a towel from the counter and wiped at the wet spots. "Sorry," I said.

He took my hand and stilled it against his chest. I looked up at him. He dipped his head and brushed his lips over mine in a gentle kiss. If someone had been watching, they might have described it as chaste, but chaste was the last thing I felt as the sizzle went straight from my mouth all the way down to my lady bits.

"I'm not sorry," he said. Parker eased himself back from me. He grabbed his windbreaker off the back of the small sofa. He gave me a half-smile. "I'm going to go now, before you say something that will ruin this moment for me." It was said teasingly, but I could feel and scent that he meant every single word.

I didn't argue. "Good night, Parker."

He nodded to me and opened the door. "Good night, Lily."

Renee George

CHAPTER TWELVE

THE NEXT MORNING, I called my friend Hazel. She was the chief of police back in our hometown, but she'd also been an investigator in the FBI for a decade before that, and I wanted her to reach out to her contacts for some information for me.

"Hey, Lils," Haze said brightly. "What's up?"

"I found a body."

"Another one? What are you, a murder magnet?"

"Har har." I could hear Tizzy in the background going on about what flowers would be in season in June. "What's that about June?"

"Ford and I have finally set a wedding date."

"Oh, Haze, I'm so happy for you!" It was a bright spot on a cold day. "What day? I don't want to miss it for anything."

"You'd better not. I can't get married without my maid of honor."

My emotions swelled and choked off my words.

"Say yes," she said.

"Yes," I managed to croak out. "Of course I will be your maid of honor."

"Good. Now that that's settled. Tell me about this body."

"The guy's name is James Wright, and he'd been dead for a long time in the walls of the house I just bought."

"Wow. You really do stumble over the most interesting cases."

"Believe me, not by choice. This guy was wanted for bank robbery. His partner was captured and sentenced to forty years in prison."

"What do you need from me?"

"Everything you can tell me. Also, can you find out if a Merl Peterson had any connection to either of the bank robbers?"

"Your landlord?"

"He's dead too."

"Oh, Lils."

"I didn't find his body. But he died the same night I found James. I'm struggling to think it's a coincidence." I didn't tell her I got shot at because I didn't want her popping down to Moonrise and taking over. I wanted Haze's help, but on my terms, not hers.

"Okay. I've got it written down. James Wright, wanted bank robber. What was his partner's name?"

"Gail Martin."

"A woman?"

"No, a man."

"And Merl Peterson, you want any connection."

"Yes." I paused for a second then added, "And John Mills, the previous owner of this house. See if there's a connection there as well."

"Makes sense since the guy was found in his wall. Anything else?"

"That's it for right now." I changed the subject. "I'm really happy for you and Ford. I'm sure his mom is over the moon about you two getting married."

"She's got her fingers in every part of this wedding pie," Tizzy said loudly. "I think she's going to give Haze gray hair."

"Haze is strong. She'll manage, even if she has to get creative."

"Not too creative. Her magic still sucks, Lils."

I laughed. "You're right. She shouldn't get too creative."

"Is everything okay, Lily?" Haze asked. "You sound a little weird this morning."

My cheeks heated as I thought about Parker's kiss. As it was, I was a little afraid to go to work today. Would he expect me to be different with him? More intimate because of the hug and the kiss we'd shared? I didn't want to walk around on eggshells around him, but really, I'd gotten very good at avoiding him at work this past week. I could do it a few more days until I figured out what to do next.

"Call me when you get the information."

"I guess you don't want to talk about it."

"Nope."

"Love you, Lils."

"Love you back, Haze."

After I hung up, I looked down at Smooshie, who'd flopped onto the floor at my feet. "Potty time."

She leaped up and twisted around excitedly.

"It's potty time," I said again, this time with playful energy.

Her high-pitched bark immediately lightened my mood. I leaned over and lay my head on her back and scratched her hind end right above her tail. It was her joy spot. After, I went to the front door, opened it, and said, "Go forth and conquer the yard."

She jumped out the door and over the two metal steps like an antelope. I sat down on the steps, debating my next move. Did I call Parker and ask for the day off? Or did I go in to face the music?

He'd called me brave last night. In the cruel light of day, I felt like a coward. At least when it came to

Parker. I'd been kissed once or twice in my life, and definitely more thoroughly, but never had I felt the depth of connection I'd experienced when Parker's mouth whispered over mine.

I touched my lips, ghosting my fingers across as if to recapture the exact memory. "It wouldn't work," I told Smoosh, as he ran up to me and dropped a stick at my feet. I picked it up and threw it. She took off after it, but instead of bringing it back to me, she put it in one of the holes she'd dug and buried it.

"The game's no fun if you're the only one playing," I told her. There was no play in the look she gave me. It was similar to the look that Parker had given me after he'd kissed me and right before he left. Definitely not playing.

Renee George

CHAPTER THIRTEEN

I PUT MY BIG GIRL panties on and went into work. I don't know if I was relieved or disappointed when Keith told me that Parker had gone on a supply run. It took a lot to run a shelter, and it seemed no matter how much food or cleaning supplies he bought, it didn't take long to run out.

"Theresa get any more notes?" I asked Keith.

He scratched at his undeveloped beard. His eyes were a pretty aquamarine, and they turned him from goofy-looking to handsome, or at least interesting. "No, nothing. I can't convince her, but it was probably for Jock. That dude is a serious piece of waste."

I didn't disagree. "I'm sure nothing will come of it." Nothing had come of the two notes sent to me. I think the person wanted to see what kind of reactions he or she could get from the people targeted.

Shake enough trees, and you'll find a few nuts.

The front door opened and Addison Newton walked in. I gave the boy a questioning look, but said, "Hi, Addy. What can I do for you today?"

"Hey, Ms. Mason." He bounced up a little on his toes and back down. "I...do you all need some help? I'm interested in volunteering."

"Oh." His question surprised me. He didn't strike me as a charitable person when I watched him with his friends. "Why do you want to volunteer?"

"I like dogs. I think I like them more than people."

"And?"

"And I have to have some volunteer hours somewhere to qualify for the A-Plus scholarship. It's the only thing I have left to do to qualify."

"So dogs and college?"

He smiled, and it was almost shy. "Yes, ma'am."

"Write a short essay on why you want to volunteer here, and I'll convince Parker to give you a shot." I was pretty sure Parker would take him on regardless. The shelter could always use more help, but I wanted to see if the boy was serious about volunteering here, or if he just thought it was an easy way to rack of up some hours. Regardless, I was impressed he was taking the initiative to go to college.

"What kind of degree do you want?"

"I'm leaning toward doing something in physical therapy or sports medicine. I've had a few injuries playing football, and I think I'd be good at helping people rehab."

"You've given it some thought," I said.

"I have."

"Do we have a deal?"

"I'll write the essay tonight," he said. He rubbed his hand over his hair in a way that was meant to be aw-shucks charming. And it was.

"Then I'll see you tomorrow."

Come lunchtime, Parker still hadn't come back from his outing. I walked the few blocks to The Cat's Meow to clear my head on the way. It was unusually slow, but weekdays could get that way for Buzz. He said he didn't mind, because it all worked out in the wash on the weekends, and breakfast was busy every day.

Opal and Pearl sat at their usual table. I swear there had to be roots growing from their booties to the cushioned seats.

"Hey, Lily," Pearl said. "I heard you found a mummy at your new place."

I looked over at Buzz through the kitchen window. He shrugged unhelpfully.

Freda said, "Mind your business, Pearl. Lily's got enough on her plate right now." When she was closer to me, she said, "I heard you almost got shot again last night. I'm glad you're okay."

"Thanks," I said. I glared at Buzz again, and again, he shrugged.

"Can I come back?" I asked.

"Sure," he said. "I'm just cleaning the grills. They can wait a few minutes." He looked at Freda. "Holler if we get someone. I'll be back in the office."

Buzz's office was a small room, minimally furnished with a desk, a desk chair, and a wooden chair in front of it for people he met with. There was a filing cabinet and a floor safe as well, but that was it. I sat in the wooden chair. He perched on the corner of the desk.

"I heard about last night from Nadine," he said. "How come you didn't call me?"

"By the time I left the sheriff's, I just wanted to go home."

"I get it," he said. "Do you think you were targeted?"

"I don't know. I was...preoccupied when I left Dally's. I didn't notice anyone following or watching me. It could have been someone just messing around and the gun accidentally went off, but I'm scared it was a warning."

"Why?"

"First I find a body, then my landlord is murdered, and then someone takes a shot at me. One event by itself wouldn't raise my alarms, but all of them together seem too big not to be connected.

Nadine had already told him about the bank robbers. He rubbed my shoulder. "Are you all right?"

"Other than getting tired of people asking me that question, I'm fine." I sounded curter than I meant to be. "I'm sorry I didn't text you back last night. I just didn't want to even think about it anymore."

"Parker came by for breakfast this morning," Buzz said.

I glanced at Buzz. "Yeah, so. He comes here for breakfast all the time."

He gave me an appraising look. "But he usually doesn't come in with your scent all over him. What changed?"

"Nothing." I stood up because I suddenly felt restless. Pent up. Caged. "Nothing has changed. At least not for me."

"You're lying to yourself, Lily."

"It's none of your business."

"If it's anyone's business, it's mine. I'm the only one in town you can be completely honest with. You can tell me anything, and I'll listen."

"You'll judge," she said unfairly. Buzz was the only person in town she could talk to, and he'd done nothing but help her since she'd arrived in Moonrise.

"Maybe. But only because you're family. That's what family does." He smiled. "We love, we judge, but ultimately, we accept."

Family also left. That's what Buzz had done when my mother and father mated. He'd left. He'd been in love with my mom and couldn't stand to see his brother take her as his wife. Buzz's real name was Daniel, the same as my brother's name. It meant even though my parents never told us about Buzz, they missed him enough to name their only son after him.

"I care about Parker more than I should. More than I can stand if I can't be honest with him. It's easier just to keep my distance."

Buzz hiked his brows. "How's that working out so far?"

"Terrible, but it's better than the alternative."

"You mean it's better to be alone and lonely, instead of with someone who makes you happy."

"For now."

"What?"

"Happy for now. It can't last. He'll get older, and I won't age much. One day he'll notice, and he'll wonder why. And even if I trusted him enough to tell him the truth, he'd grow old and die right before my very eyes. I'd be helpless to do anything more than watch life take him away from me."

"So better to be miserable than allow yourself real happiness for a decade, maybe more."

"I can't give him children. Is it really fair for me to take away his best years, just so I don't have to be alone? He needs someone who he can grow with. That's not me. I'll stay still, and he'll pass me by, and I will have robbed him of a chance for real happiness."

"Who's to say it would even last? You guys could have a few good dates, and then a big fight would end it all. Or you might get hit by a bus a year or two from now, and he would then outlive *you*. The world is full of what ifs and would've-could'ves. You have to take every day as a chance to eke out some happiness for yourself."

I stared at Buzz. "The human be damned, as long as we get ours. Is that what you're saying?"

"Do you think that's how I feel about Nadine?"

"Don't you?" I sounded harsh even to my own ears.

Buzz's expression was a mixture of hurt and disbelief. "I love her," he said softly. "Does she seem unhappy to you?"

"Not yet." Goddess, what was wrong with me? When had I become such a snipe? Oh, about the same time my heart got so twisted by a human who would never be my true mate that I couldn't see straight.

He shook his head. "Well, there's the family judging thing we talked about."

I should have apologized, but I couldn't bring myself to do it. I'd felt isolated most my life, but when you want ice cream, but no one makes it, you get to the point where you realize going without ice cream is a just a fact of life. Parker was ice cream. Ice cream that wanted me as much as I wanted it. Only, I was pretending to be lactose intolerant. Argh. "I've got to go."

"You haven't eaten lunch."

"I've lost my appetite."

"Fine," Buzz said.

"Fine." I walked out of his office, past the kitchen and out into the dining area.

Freda said, "You gonna eat, hon?"

"Not today, Freda."

On the way out the door, I ran into the guy who'd been arguing with Jeff Callahan. Literally.

He was holding a stack of folders and not watching as he walked through the door, and I'd been distracted as well. "I'm so sorry," I said, and knelt to help him pick up his work.

"It's okay. My fault," he offered. "I should have been watching."

"Me too." I smiled.

He smiled back, as if really noticing me for the first time.

"I'm Lily Mason." I held out my hand. He shook it.

"I'm Gary. Gary Ream."

"Do you always take your work to lunch, Gary?"

"Not usually."

"Would you like some company?"

"That'd be nice," he said. "Yes, I'd like that."

Freda gave me a strange look. I ignored her. I could change my mind about eating if I wanted. Gary and I sat in the nearest booth to the door.

"What'll you have?" Freda asked.

"A tuna melt, salad, and a diet cola," Gary said.

"I'll take the double-bacon cheeseburger with cowboy chips, a side of smoky beans, and a regular cola."

Gary's eyes widened.

"I like to eat," I said.

Freda said, "Separate checks?"

I rolled my eyes. "Yes, please."

"No," Gary insisted. "I'll get Ms. Mason's lunch today."

Freda went to turn in our orders and get our drinks. I turned my attention to Gary. "So, what is it that you do?"

"I'm the circuit court clerk."

"What do you do there?'

"I mostly fill out a lot of paperwork." He laughed again. "I make sure all the ducks are in a row for the courts and a lot more."

"Like what?"

"Small claims. Child-support enforcement. That kind of thing."

I smiled. "So you go after deadbeat dads, huh?"

"Not just dads," he said. "I had to serve a mother's work that we would be garnishing her wages if she didn't pay her ex-husband child support."

"Wow." I had a feeling this guy knew a lot about the seedier side of some people in this county. "What about property auctions?"

"I oversee some of that too."

"I just bought a house and some property that had gone up for auction."

"Really? I don't remember your name. I have a pretty good memory for these things."

"Well, technically, Merl Peterson won the auction, but he sold me the place after."

"Poor Merl," Gary said. "He was one of the good ones. I can't believe he's gone."

I don't know what I expected from Gary, but sympathy for Merl wasn't it. The man across from me looked genuinely sad. "Were you all friends?"

"For many years," Gary said. "I was shocked to hear about his death."

Freda walked over and set our drinks down. "Food will be out in a jiffy," she said.

"Merl owned several properties. Which one did you get?" Gary asked.

I took a sip of my cola and kept my eyes on his face. I wasn't getting any signs he was hiding anything. Not yet, anyways. "It's off of DD Road, 1031 northwest 400 Road."

Gary blanched.

"You know where that is?"

"Yes." He tugged at his tie, loosening it from his throat. "Is it hot in here?"

"Yes," I told him, and leaned forward. "I heard Jeff Callahan had been interested in the place. Do you know why?" I thought about how much I wanted him to tell me the truth.

"He wants to parse out the acres and turn the property into a housing subdivision." Gary put his hand to his mouth as if he couldn't believe what just came out. "I...I...that information is confidential, Lily. I hope you'll keep it to yourself."

"No worries, Gary." Bummer. I had been hoping for more nefarious reasons. I couldn't see anyone getting murdered to build houses, but motives could be tricky. And who good was his business? If I'd learned nothing from The Learning Channel, I'd learned property development wasn't cheap. Callahan had wreaked of marijuana when I'd met him. Not generally the drug of choice for he ambitious, but one never knew.

"Thank you for your honesty. I appreciate it."

He mumbled, "You're welcome," just as Freda brought our lunches over.

"Yum," I said. I wanted to go back to ask Buzz about Jeff Callahan, but I was still irritated about our conversation. I nodded at Gary's cute little tuna melt and garden salad and picked up my giant double cheeseburger. "Dig in."

I looked out the window. Adam Davis was standing out on the sidewalk in front of the diner talking to Ryan. They were talking and laughing. I knocked on the window and they both startled. I smirked. Ryan waved me to come out, but I wasn't finished with my burger.

Gary got up, his tuna sandwich half eaten and his salad untouched. "Good day, Miss Mason." He made a beeline for the register.

I motioned Ryan inside. He and Adam came in and sat down in the booth with me. Freda was over in seconds. She cleared Gary's plate and took drink orders from Adam and Ryan.

"What are you two up to today?" I asked.

Ryan leaned forward. "Well, I was just heading back to my office when I ran into Beast Mode here."

Adam chuckled. "That's right. I haven't seen Big Sexy since he left for college."

"Big Sexy and Beast Mode? Do tell me more."

"Our freshman year, Ryan was the tallest guy in our class," Adam said. "All the girls were constantly throwing themselves at him. One of the senior football players nicknamed him Big Sexy and it stuck."

"And Beast Mode?"

Adam grinned. "Just look at me, darling. My junior year, I had a growth spurt and bulked up big time." He and Ryan both said at the same time, "Beast Mode Cowboy." Then they hooted.

I shook my head and laughed. "Did all of you have nicknames or just you two?"

"Our Lily wants to know about Parker," Ryan said.

I gave him a warning look. He smirked.

"We called Parker, The Gun Show. The guy had biceps that looked like two cantaloupes when he flexed his muscles."

I barked a laugh. Thinking about Parker as a high school boy flexing his muscles was such a departure from the way he was now. "And the others?"

Ryan said, "Mike was The Duffster. Jeff was The Nerdist."

"Poor Jeff."

"He didn't mind." Adam shook his head. "He's really changed."

"How so?" I asked. I finished my burger and cowboy chips, and was working on my smoky beans.

"He just isn't the same guy I used to know." His brow ridge was predominant, and his eyebrows furrowed over the thickness. He looked at Ryan and said, "And Mark, what was it we used to call him?"

"I don't remember," Ryan said.

"Sparkles!" Adam said. "Markles Sparkles." He laughed.

"Yeah, that was it." Ryan sounded miserable. They'd been close friends. I wondered what changed that. Age and distance, I supposed. It had a way turning friends into strangers.

CHAPTER FOURTEEN

WHEN I GOT BACK to work, Keith told me that Parker had come back but went out again to assess a couple who wanted to become fosters for rescue dogs. It looked like I was going to dodge an emotional bullet with him today. Was I disappointed? Maybe.

Theresa Simmons walked into the shelter near the end of my shift. She gave me a brief hug. "Lily, how are you feeling today? I heard you almost got shot last night. How terrible!"

"I thought you had the day off," I told her. "Thanks for covering for me yesterday. I really appreciate it."

"You've had such an awful week. My mom said that Dad hasn't slept hardly at all since Merl Peterson was found. They were friends, you know."

"I didn't know. Merl was a nice man."

"He really was. He didn't have any kids or a wife. It's sad that he doesn't have anyone to mourn him. I guess Greer is making the arrangements for his funeral."

"Greer?" Parker had said they were good friends, even so, most of the time family took care of those kinds of arrangements.

"Yes, he's the executor for Merl's estate. Merl already had his plot and stuff paid for, but Greer is taking care of everything else."

"Parker didn't tell me." I felt bad I hadn't reached out to Greer since Merl had been killed. Greer was the only reason Merl even considered selling the house and land to me.

"Just between you and me, Jock says that Merl left the bulk of his estate to the Moosehead Lodge. It's a tidy sum."

"How much?"

Her eyes lit up. "Over a million dollars in cash and properties."

"That's a tidy sum."

She grinned. "Right?"

"So he didn't have any family?"

"He had a sister who died six years ago from breast cancer." Theresa shook her head somberly. "She had a son from her first marriage. But Merl wasn't close to him. At least that's what my dad says."

Sheriff Avery sure did a lot of talking around the dinner table. I wondered if he knew just how much Theresa liked to gossip. He definitely wouldn't like the fact that she was sharing all the personal information with me.

"He must have been a lonely man."

"Not hardly," Theresa said. "He was completely immersed in the lodge. Plus his friends took turns inviting him around for dinners and such. I'd never seen anyone so content with their life." A wistful expression crossed her face. Her tone turned bitter. "He stayed busy during the day, and at night he got to go home to a quiet house without anyone bossing him around or making him feel like the worst scum humanity has to offer."

I couldn't help but think about Theresa's husband Jock. Did he make her feel like the worst scum of humanity? "I'm sorry, Theresa."

Her expression changed from angry to blank before she allowed a smile to light her face up again. "For what?" she asked, doing a decent job at hiding her personal pain.

I gave her hand a squeeze. "Thank you again for working for me yesterday."

"For you…" she said, "…any time."

****

Renee George

I drove to The Rusty Wrench, which was two streets over from Parker's place. Greer had his garage door open and a Volkswagon Beetle up on the rack. I parked. Smooshie saw Greer in his coveralls by a monitor just inside the garage, and she excitedly barked.

"Excited to see the G-paw," I said. "Just hold tight." I clipped her leash onto her collar.

Greer craned his head back and smiled.

I got out of the truck, Smooshie in tow. Well, more like she was towing me. "She can't wait to see you, Greer." I laughed as he fished a treat out of his pocket.

"Sit," he told her.

Smooshie obediently sat. She looked up at him with love and expectation.

"Good girl," Greer said. He put his palm out and Smooshie took the nibble, happily chomping away.

"She really loves you."

"Then my plan is working," he said. Although he was smiling, I could see the exhaustion on his face. His skin looked a little duller, the lines around his eyes a little deeper. Greer's hair was graying. When I first moved here, I'd never really spent much time with humans before, so I thought he must be really old to have gray hair, but it turned out Greer was forty-eight. Which meant, he was only thirteen years older than me. It put a lot into perspective for me.

"I'm really sorry about Merl," I said. "I know you two were close. I hate that this happened to him."

Greer's blue eyes were stormy. "Why would anyone want to kill Merl? He would give you the shirt off his back. Everyone who knew Merl liked him. He was that kind of guy."

"How did you two become friends?"

"When Amy died, I started attending grief counseling. Merl was in my group."

That's right. Merl and Greer were both widows. I hated that I was dredging up the painful past and the painful present all at the same time. "So, you can't think of anyone who'd want to hurt him?"

"Not a soul."

Smooshie got on the trail of something that led her in circles around my legs. I braced myself to keep from falling when she wrapped us up tight, and then turned to get unwrapped.

Greer smiled. "I'm glad you stopped by, Lily. You always make the day a little brighter." He patted Smooshie on the head, and she sniffed his hand for more treats. "Both of you."

"I'm glad. I should have come by sooner. It's been a crazy week."

"Yeah, I heard about the body in your wall. I can't believe you're staying out there after that.

Parker would gladly put you up for a while longer until things get sorted. You guys make a good team."

All Greer needed to add to the end of that sentence to make it any more blatant was a nod-nod-wink-wink. "I know he would let me stay as long as I needed, but I have to have my own place. My own space. You understand, right?"

"Not really," Greer said. "I'd give anything to not have my own space again."

He put his hands in his coveralls. Smooshie sat and readied herself for a treat. Not this time, I thought.

"I didn't mean to be careless with my words, Greer."

"I know you didn't."

"I came by for a little work as well."

"You have truck problems again? Martha ran great at her checkup last month."

"She's still running good. I wanted you to take a look at a hole in the door frame on the driver side."

"How'd that happen?"

I guess Parker didn't tell his dad everything. Hopefully that meant he hadn't told his dad about our middle-of-the-night kiss. I didn't want Greer getting dreamy for a wedding. "Someone shot it last night."

Surprise replaced sadness in his expression. "What idiot did that?"

"You tell me and we'll both know. The police didn't find him last night. He shot once and took off."

Greer walked with me out to the truck and looked at the damage. He put his finger inside the hole. "I can pull it out, seal it and paint it. It doesn't look like it hit anything important. I'd say it was a .22 hole and probably shot from a good distance, since it didn't penetrate more than the body."

"Is that significant?"

"Not really. It was probably some kids."

"Why do you say that?"

"Kids can be dumb. Like shooting-a-gun-in-town kind of dumb. And a .22 has the cheapest rounds to fire. It was probably a case of accidental stupidity that got your truck shot."

"Do I detect personal experience in your observation?"

He grinned. "I might have shot out a light or three when I was young." He narrowed his gaze at me. "Don't go telling Parker on me though. I'm happy for the boy to think I've never been anything but perfect."

I laughed, locked my mouth, and then threw away the key. "Can I leave Martha with you tomorrow morning? I can pick her up after work."

"Sure, and if I don't get it finished, just drop her back again on the next day you're at the shelter."

"That will be Saturday."

"You're not going to the sport's banquet with Parker?"

"No." I tried for incredulous and failed miserably. "I'm going to watch the shelter for him while he goes. Why would you think I'd be going?"

"I thought he might take you as a date."

"He's going with Naomi Wells." Saying her name made me feel surly.

Greer shook his head. "I told you kids are dumb."

****

I had to get home. Nick Newton had called. He said he could come out this evening and look at the place for me. It was the soonest he could work it into his schedule, and I wasn't about to say no. Mark Stephens was coming out to look at the wiring as well. If I could get electricity going to the house, it would make the work a little easier.

Nick arrived in a white pickup that had a sticker on the door panel with the words "Handy Contractors" and a website and phone number. The bed had a large metal toolbox near the back window. Mark pulled in right after him. His truck was red, no label.

"Hi, Nick. Mark," I said when they got out of their trucks. Smooshie said hello by ramming her wide head between Nick's thighs.

Nick wobbled back as I grabbed Smooshie by the collar. "She aggressive?"

"With her love," I said. "I'll put her in the trailer while you work."

"What's going on with your yard?" There were five or six holes now in the yard, a couple deeper than the others.

"She likes to dig. I think there's a gopher or something underground, and she's not going to rest until she finds it."

"You should break her of that."

I liked Nick, but I didn't want his advice on how to treat my pittie. "She's fine. I don't really mind, and if she's happy, who does it hurt?"

"All right." He shrugged. He put on a toolbelt he'd grabbed from his passenger seat. "I'll go ahead and get started."

"Thanks, I really appreciate this." I looked at Mark, who carried a bag with some equipment, most likely voltage testers and such.

"No problem. Happy to help," Nick said perfunctorily.

"Me too," added Mark.

I put Smooshie up and joined the two men in the house. The police had done a number on my walls in the living room. I sighed. More money. More work. I wondered if I had dreamed too big, thinking I could get this place livable. I imagined myself twenty years from now still living in Buzz's trailer while this place rotted to the ground.

"Is this where they found the body?" Mark asked, pointing to a side wall. He hadn't changed much from his high school pictures. Still a nice-looking guy, maybe a little thicker in body, but he had a wide mouth, angled cheekbones, and soft brown eyes that contrasted with his short blond hair in a way that made him look interesting.

"No," I said and gestured to the wall across from me. "In there."

"That's the darnedest thing I've ever heard of." Nick shook his shoulders. "Gives me the willies."

"Me too," I said. "Do you know who put up the walls in here?"

Mark shrugged, but I didn't expect him to know. He had left Moonrise his senior year, before the body had been put there.

Nick ran his hand down an intact seam. "Too rough to be professional. It's not bad, though."

It wasn't exactly a lie, but it didn't smell completely of the truth either. "Well, whoever did it packed a corpse inside. Is there a way to find out who?"

"Unless it was a professional contractor, probably not. Lots of people do this kind of work under the table. They get paid in cash, no paper trail."

Mark nodded. "Lots of high school students get hired for summer work and such. Though I can't imagine anyone killing someone and sticking them in the wall." He shivered as if the idea repulsed him. "I best get started. Sarah wants me home for dinner by six. My folks are coming over." I could detect a whiff of acrid distain when he talked about his parents. He wasn't happy about seeing them.

I left Mark to do his thing with the fuse box and the outlets and followed Nick around the house. We went room to room, even upstairs. I wanted to take down several of the upstairs walls and create a large bedroom-slash-sanctuary for myself up there. The windows gave a bird's-eye view to the beautiful surroundings.

"Your roof is pretty good. Mills must have had that replaced not too long back. There are a few water stains, but nothing fresh, and with the storm the other night, this place would have leaked like a sieve if the roof hadn't held up."

"That's great news." Less money. Less work. "Do you think I could tear down some walls up here? I'd like to combine the two bedrooms and make them into one big one."

"You can take out the inside walls if you leave the one that runs down the middle here. It goes down into the inside corner of the living room, and," he made a straight-line swing with his arm, "leave the beams up going that way, on both top and bottom. Those are important to keeping your upstairs upstairs and the room over your head." He grinned.

"Gotcha."

"You can wall up the second bedroom door, and it wouldn't be hard to open up the space to the upstairs bathroom as well. Just remember, the thicker the beam at the end of the wall or if you run into a metal girder, don't try to take it out. You can always call me if you have a question."

"Do you have a smartphone?"

"It's smarter than me, but yes."

"You may be getting some texted pictures from me," I said.

He laughed. "Keep them clean or the old lady will have my 'nads."

I laughed. "They'll probably be dirty, but only in a dust-and-cobweb kind of way."

"Deal," he said.

I went downstairs to find Mark. He was in the living room looking inside the walls where they were open. He had a flashlight and was looking toward the base of the wall.

"Is there wiring down there?"

He jumped a little.

"I didn't mean to startle you."

"It's okay." Mark took a deep breath. "I don't see any electrical lines on this wall. You might want to run some before you replace the walls. Some outlets over here will be convenient."

"Thanks. I'll do that." Mark still seemed a little shaken. I hadn't meant to sneak up on him. He gave me a shakey laugh.

"How come you moved away?"

"It's a long story," he said while he moved around the room.

"I've got time."

He gave me a tight smile. "My parents decided I needed a change of scenery."

It wasn't a complete lie, but it wasn't the whole truth. Why would his parents send him away? Was this the reason for the change in his scent when he talked about them?

"And you came back?"

"My wife and I wanted to be in a small town to raise our kids. And since my parents were still here..." He shrugged again. "I don't think you'll have too many problems with the electricity over here. The fuse box is in good shape, and it looks like the outlets have been updated over the years. I didn't see any loose wires in the exposed walls. It's a little harder to tell on the plaster ones, but I think you'll be fine."

"You think?"

He smiled. "If things spark, shut it down."

I smiled remembering lunch with his friends. "Sparkles."

Mark's smile faded fast. "What's that?"

Ouch. "I'm sorry. Ryan and Adam said your nickname had been Markles Sparkles in high school. You're an electrician. I thought it was fitting."

I watched his fist clench at the mention of of Ryan and his nickname. Sheesh. They must have had a serious falling out for him to react with so much anger.

Mark narrowed his eyes on me, but Nick came down the stairs and put a stop to whatever he was going to say.

Nick tapped his clipboard. "I'll write up a few things that I noticed, Lily. Just remember —"

"If it's thick, metal, or connected to a joist, leave it alone." I looked at the wall of the living room he told me to leave alone. "And don't take down the beams in this wall."

Nick winked and nodded. "You got it." Nick and Mark left together, and I went to the trailer to fix some dinner for Smoosh and me.

My phone beeped. There was a message from Reggie. I'd forgot that I'd exchanged numbers with her last night when we'd been waiting for the police to arrive after the shooting. I clicked on it. There was a picture attached, and the message said, *this was in his hand.*

I clicked on the picture to download it to my phone. It was a large file and came up slowly. When it finally downloaded, it was showed a rectangular bar with the number 400 engraved in the middle. My house was on 400 road? Was this a coincidence? Or did the number have something to do with my address?

I texted her back. *Weird.*

Right?

What is it?

Some kind of pin, I think. Two prongs on the backside.

What does the number mean?

Your guess is as good as mine.

Thanks. Talk to you soon.

Welcome. Don't tell anyone you got this from me. Remember, snitches get stitches, and since I'm the doctor...

I laughed. LOL. Mum's the word.

I tried to think about what I knew for sure. I still didn't know if the two deaths were connected, but I had a gut feeling. Merl was an upstanding guy in the community. Everyone liked and respected him. James Wright was a low-life criminal. He wasn't even from this area. I had a niggling feeling that the pieces to the puzzle were mostly there, but I just didn't know how to put them together.

I half thought I'd get another visit from Parker, considering he'd shown up two days in a row, but everything was quiet. I threw two twelve-ounce steaks in a hot cast iron skillet. The sizzling meat perked Smooshie right up. She was suddenly very interested in what I was doing.

"I'll share a little," I told her. She liked her dog food better when I minced up freshly cooked meat and mixed it in. I had to be careful though, because Ryan warned me that she was at a healthy weight, but if she gained any more pounds it wouldn't be good for her. The last thing I wanted to do was hurt Smooshie by overindulging her.

My phone rang as I flipped them over to caramelize the other side. I picked it up. "Haze, what do you have for me?"

"Hi, Lily. I'm fine. How are you? Good? So nice to hear it."

"Hi, Haze, how are you?" I asked. "You sound great. Now give."

"Fine. Your boy James Wright doesn't have any connection to the area, but his prison pal, Gail Martin, used to live in that area with his mom and stepdad. A Nancy and Darrel Shephard."

"Do they still live in the area?"

"Nope. Martin left home in 1982. His parents abandoned their place, and pretty much disappeared around 1984. They resurfaced a few years later when the stepfather was caught pulling a con. He was using an alias at the time. Fingerprints matched him to his real name though."

"Did they have any ties to Merl Peterson?"

"Nothing I could find."

"Well, crap."

Still. Her voice sounded too excited for this kind of news. "What else did you find out?"

"Ask me where the Shephards and their juvenile delinquent son lived?"

My stomach turned. "Seriously?"

"No lie, my friend. 1031 NW 400 Road. Your place."

"Goddess help me. Is Martin still in prison?" Had he been released early? Escaped? I was jumping to conclusions, but a freaking bank robber with con-man parents had lived here at one time, and I'd found his partner in the wall.

"He's still in. The police never found the money he stole. One and a half million dollars."

I whistled. I lived in a trailer and could barely afford my mortgage. One and a half million dollars was an astronomical amount of money.

"He's not even eligible for parole because of that. You have another ten years before you have to start worrying about that jailbird."

"Thanks, Haze. I don't know if any of this helps yet, but I'll keep you up-to-date."

"Lily."

"Yeah?"

"Stay safe."

"I will. I promise." It was a promise I hoped I could keep.

CHAPTER FIFTEEN

PARKER DIDN'T CALL or stop by the night before, and I was a little disappointed. I thought he would at least call me. Was he avoiding me? Was the kiss so bad, he was living with regrets?

I had an aching pit inside me when I drove to town in the morning. I wanted to go by the college before work. My purpose was twofold. First, I was going to pick up an application from the Admissions office, and second, I wanted to talk to Jeff Callahan. I'd checked his class schedule online, and he had a nine a.m. class on Fridays.

I pulled into the large parking lot. Cars, trucks, and vans with red college tags filled in almost every available space in both the student and faculty parking. Luckily, I was only a visitor this morning. There were a handful of open spots, and I parked Martha in one at the end of the first row.

It wasn't cold, but I pulled my cardigan tighter around me. I didn't expect to be nervous, but what if I couldn't get into the GED program? When Hazel had given me forged identity documents that put my age at twenty-eight, I should have had her get me a high school diploma as well. My nerves were making my hands shake. Ugh. So much for Brave Lily.

I walked into the Administration Building. There was a room guide on the wall. Admissions was in room 109a. I walked down the wide corridor, avoiding eye contact. The office had a glass front with a glass door. Inside there were three employees, two women and one man, sitting behind a long counter. It reminded me of a trip to the DMV. There weren't any numbers to grab, so I opened the door and went in without ceremony.

The first woman, a full-figured brunette with hazel-brown eyes and a creamy complexion, looked up at me and said, "Hi, what can I do for you today?"

I froze for a second.

"This is Admissions. Are you in the right room?"

"I think so." Why was I so embarrassed to admit I never finished high school?

I glanced nervously at the other two clerks. The other woman was a stern-looking black woman who kept giving me side eye over her reading glasses. The man was a thin and balding with pasty skin from too much fluorescent lighting and not enough sun, if I had to guess. He wore a beige short-sleeve, button-down shirt with a pocket protector in his front pocket. He had glasses too, but his were for distance, and magnified his eyes in a way that made them look buggy.

"Don't mind Al and Tilda. They love to scare incoming freshman. This will be your first time enrolling, correct?"

Tilda looked at her coworker and said, "You're ruining my fun, Gladys."

I took a deep breath and pulled my ovaries up by the bootstraps. I am a strong woman and a Shifter. I ain't afraid of no GED. "I never finished high school. I'd like to enroll for your HSE class." HSE stood for high school equivalency.

"That's great," Tilda said. "Good for you, honey."

Al grumbled something about the fall of today's youth, and shuffled to the copier with a folder stuffed with papers.

"Don't mind him," Gladys said. "Al is one of those people who came out of the womb grouchy." She opened her drawer and pulled out a map of the campus. She pointed to a square on the map. "You're here." She drew a line with her finger to a building that was back behind the square. "You need to be here in the Tolliver Building. Enrollment starts next week on Tuesday, Wednesday, and Friday, between nine a.m. and four p.m. in the Learning Center. You come back then and check in over there and they will get you set up for a summer course."

The way she rattled off the information told me I wasn't the only one who came to the wrong place for the program. "Thank you, Gladys. Is there anything I should bring along? I have my driver's license and a birth certificate."

"Then you'll be fine," she said reassuringly.

"Do you know how much it costs?"

"Absolutely nothing." She smiled.

Tilda chuckled. "It's an investment."

"Lily," a woman said from the doorway. "What are you doing over here?"

I turned, a snarl on my lips. Naomi Wells was dressed in a cream-colored pant suit with blood-red heels and a black and red hand bag. Her hair was done up in a flattering French roll. Her makeup was as flawless as her outfit.

Did I hate her because she was pretty? I'd never been jealous of other women before. When growing up in a town with witches, you get used to being one of the ugly ducklings. Was it just because she was putting the moves on Parker? Maybe. I didn't want to think of myself as petty and jealous.

I tried to make my face pleasant and relaxed. Her smirk told me I was failing miserably.

"Hi, Naomi. I'm just—"

Gladys stood up and handed me a folder with Course Catalog written on the front. "Here is the information you wanted." She gave me a quick wink. "Hope to see you again soon."

I nodded gratefully. "This is a small room," I said to Naomi. "Let's take it out into the hall."

When we exited Admissions, Naomi said, "What do you want to study?"

I looked down at the course catalog in my hand. "Oh, uhm, something in medicine. What are you doing here?"

"I..." She gave me an odd look. "I can't think of what I was about to say."

Was Naomi hiding something? My witch inheritance made me an honesty magnet, but if someone really didn't want me to know something, they might not be able to lie to me, but they could avoid telling the truth. Naomi was telling the truth about not being able to remember what she was going to say, because she had been about to tell a lie, but instead, the real reason for her visit to the college was on her lips.

I pressed a little. Not too much though. "I seem to be running into you everywhere. I'm going to start thinking you're following me." I lightened my tone and asked. "You're not stalking me, are you, Naomi?"

"Yes," she said, then snapped her mouth shut and blinked.

Holy crap on a cracker. I never expected her admit to stalking me. I'd been feeling a little paranoid about her since she'd recorded our bathroom conversation, but what is it they say, it's not paranoia if someone is really out to get you?

"Seriously? You're following me?"

Naomi frowned. "I mean, well, nothing. I have to go." Her smile turned feral and malicious. "I can't wait to see Parker tomorrow night. I always had a thing for him in high school, but he only had eyes for Bridgette back then."

This woman loved to bring up this nightmare blast from my past. I picked my cell phone out of my purse. It was nine forty-five. Jeff Callahan's class would be over soon. "It was nice to see you, Naomi."

"I hope I'll see you around soon," she said.

Not if I see you first. "Sure," I told. "Talk to you later."

I waited for her to clack down the hall and out of sight before I made a beeline to the building's side entrance. Jeff taught in the Sanders Math and Science Building. The campus was small, so it was a short walk past the art building and the college bookstore.

I went inside, dodging a gaggle of students exiting rooms on both sides of the hall. Some classes were still full and in progress, but I knew Jeff's class was only fifty minutes. I scanned the hallway, catching the scent of pot. Unfortunately, Jeff wasn't the only recreational user on campus, and I ended up following five dead ends before I found Jeff at his instructor's desk talking to a young male student. I waited outside the door for the kid to leave.

When the room was clear, I stuck my head in the door. "Hey, Jeff."

He glanced up, clear surprise in his expression. "Lily. Hi. How are you?" He shook his head. "What are you doing out here?"

"Checking out the campus. I'm thinking about taking some classes."

"Come in," he said. "I'm just taking care of some last-minute work before I have to vacate for the next class. Chemistry starts at ten, and Professor Robins gets touchy if I don't get out of here on time."

"Don't let me stop you."

He started typing into his computer. "I just have to log attendance and sign out. I stopped using class time to do it. Some of my students need every minute of math they can get."

I would probably be one of those students. English, science, and history were easy for me, but when it came to numbers, my mind didn't always work like it should. "I might need some help with math if I decide to attend."

"My door is always open. Metaphorically speaking; I don't really have a door here, or an office. Adjunct professors pretty much share different classrooms, and we have to make arrangements if a student wants to see us before or after class." He closed the attendance window and logged off. "How are you settling in at the Mills place?"

"I like to think of it as the Mason place now."

"That's right." He smiled. "Awful business out there."

"Yeah. Talk about a surprise. I mean, I really thought mold would be the worst thing I'd find in the walls."

He laughed nervously. "I bet."

"And poor Merl Peterson."

"Right." Jeff shook his head again. "It's such a shock. Merl would give the shirt off his back to help a stranger."

He wasn't the first one to say so. And I knew from experience how true that statement was. Merl had really cut me a solid deal. "I didn't know him well, but he was certainly fair with me."

Jeff gathered up his books into a leather satchel and slung it on his shoulder. "We better go."

I walked out of the class with him. We passed a tall, thin elderly woman with long, puffy white hair, and round spectacles. She wore a very bohemian maxi dress.

"Mr. Callahan," she said in greeting.

"Professor Robins," Jeff said. "Have a nice day."

She didn't reply.

"That's the chemistry professor, huh?"

"Yes."

"I'd be scared of her too." I smiled.

Jeff smiled, but he still looked worried.

I didn't know how to work the auction into the conversation subtly. So I went for not so subtle. "Did you try to buy my house and property?"

He stopped and stared at me. "Why do you ask?" He popped a rubber band on his wrist. When I gave him a questioning look, he said, "Quitting smoking."

I didn't ask if he was talking cigarettes or marijuana, because I could smell the faint hint of weed smoke on his jacket. That alone didn't mean much. Smoke had a tendency to cling for a long time regardless of its source, but his pupils were a little dialated as well.

I kept my focus on the property. "I heard through the grapevine that you might be interested in turning the place into a housing subdivision. Bringing the suburbs to a rural address."

His expression relaxed. "Oh. You've been talking to Gary Ream." He nodded and started walking again. "Sure, I thought it would be a good investment. You win some, you lose some."

His shift from nervous to relaxed instantly increased my suspicions. "Was there another reason you wanted to buy the place?"

"I...I don't want to..." Jeff's expression became muddled confusion. I was pressing too hard in an area he didn't want to delve. He popped the rubber bands again.

"Did you kill Merl?"

He blinked. "No. Of course I didn't. Why would you even ask that?"

Another notion hit me. "What brand of cigarettes do you smoke?"

"Uh, I don't know what this had to do with--?"

"Have you been digging around on my land?"

His eyes widened, and he quickened his pace.

"You have, haven't you?" It had to be about the robbery. The money. Had he killed James Wright? He would have been, what? Seventeen at the time. It felt like a stretch, but I didn't know what else to assume. "What are you looking for out there?"

Red-faced, he practically ran out of the building with me right on his heels. Deputy Morris and Nadine, both in full uniform, were walking toward us. I looked at Nadine and when our eyes locked, she waved her hand away from her side and mouthed the word, *move away*.

There was nothing but grass to my right, so I walked in that direction when I heard Nadine shout, "On your knees, Callahan. Now."

What the heck was happening? I looked over at Jeff, who reluctantly went to his knees. He glanced my way, real fear coloring his expression.

Deputy Morris said, "Jeffrey Michael Callahan, I am placing you under arrest for the murder of Merl Peterson. You have the right to remain silent and refuse to answer questions. Anything you say may be used against you in a court of law." He put handcuffs on Jeff and stood him up. "You have the right to consult an attorney before speaking to the police, and to have an attorney present during questioning now or in the future. If you cannot afford an attorney, one will be appointed for you before any questioning, if you wish. If you decide to answer questions now without an attorney present, you will still have the right to stop answering at any time until you talk to an attorney. Knowing and understanding your rights as I have explained them to you, are you willing to answer my questions without an attorney present?"

"I don't understand any of this," Jeff said.

I knew he was being honest. He really didn't know what was happening or why.

Nadine came over as Morris took Callahan to their police SUV. "What are you doing with Jeff Callahan, Lily?"

"I just had a few questions I wanted to ask him. He'd tried to buy my property at the courthouse auction, but Merl won the bid. Do you really think he killed Merl?"

"You didn't hear this from me, but we found a bloody shirt in Jeff's trash bin. Merl's wallet was in there as well. The evidence is pretty damning."

"What made you even look at Jeff?"

"An anonymous tipster sent us in his direction."

"Who?"

Nadine frowned. "There's a reason it's called an anonymous tip."

I hadn't smelled a lie when he'd said he hadn't killed Merl. "Jeff might not be clever, but he wouldn't be smart enough to not leave any prints at the scene and then be stupid enough to leave evidence in his trash."

"One thing I know for certain, Lils." She held up her finger. "Most criminals are caught because they are careless and stupid. The shirt and wallet were wrapped in a black plastic bag and shoved to the bottom of the bin. He probably assumed when it was picked up tomorrow morning he'd be home free."

"So he conveniently put the evidence in a plastic bag to preserved it from contamination." Jeff seemed more like the type to do a more thorough job of getting rid of evidence.

"There's other evidence. Jeff phoned Merl an hour before he was murdered, and Merl was killed on campus. Jeff works here. It's looking like a pretty airtight case."

"I guess." I bit the inside of my cheek and worried it for a few seconds. "It still doesn't seem right to me. We're missing something."

Nadine looked over her shoulder and watched Morris stick Jeff in the backseat. "I got to go, Lily."

"Call me later."

"Promise," she said then sprinted to the SUV.

CHAPTER SIXTEEN

IT HAD STORMED AGAIN the night before, so I spent most of Saturday morning doing more demolition in the house. I'd really wanted to spend the evening poking around those holes to see if I could come up with more than a cigarette butt that might or might not have been Jeff's, but the soupy ground would have made it hard for me to detect any unusual scents. At least I hadn't found any more dead bodies in the house, but I didn't find any more clues either. How were a bank robber, a property developer, and an accountant tied together in such a way that would lead to murder? It came back to the money. But if there was money on this property, wouldn't someone had found it already? Maybe Jeff had. Maybe that's why he could afford to back a subdivision. Did Merl know something about the money? Could he have been blackmailing Jeff, and when the body was found, he threatened to go to the police?

It was feasible, but it still didn't feel right.

Late in the afternoon, I showered and cleaned up, including giving Smooshie a bath—she'd had no issues about wallering in the mud--, I dropped Martha off at The Rusty Wrench. Buzz said he would pick me up after work, so Greer could keep the truck a day or two if he needed it.

After, I walked over to the shelter. Smooshie had to pee every twenty feet, but eventually, we got there. I wore jeans and a sweater, my hair a little wild with frizz, and had a gut-check moment when I couldn't stop thinking about Naomi on Parker's arm. Together, they would make a handsome couple for the banquet. The quarterback and the head cheerleader. I couldn't stop the bile burn in the back of my throat.

Parker wasn't in the shelter, and I didn't know if I was relieved or disappointed. I could see his house lights on. Dang. It was disappointment. He really didn't want to see me. Paul Rogers was on duty for the afternoon shift. Addy Newton was dutifully following Paul as he worked.

I nodded to the teenager. "I see Parker approved your volunteering."

"I brought in my essay this morning and he said I could shadow Paul today, and if it works out, he'll give me more hours."

"That's great, Addy." I looked at Paul. He had been volunteering at the shelter for more than a year. The dogs always took to him right away. He was a big guy, both in height and girth, and he exuded warmth. "Is the kid doing a good job?"

"So far. He has an admirer in our new Star." Paul smiled. Star was the female we'd taken in this week. She'd been very shy with the handlers, and very submissive.

"She breaks my heart," Addy said. "I can't believe the shape she's in. If I could, I'd tear her last owner's head off."

"Ditto that," Paul said. "She's getting healthier every day though. She's put on a pound just in the last two days."

"That's great." I took my phone out of my purse and put it on Parker's desk then I put my purse in his desk drawer. "Are you leaving at six tonight?"

"Yes, but I want to take Dexter out for a run in the backyard. Addy's going to go hang out with Star for the next half hour. Tripod needs some cuddles if you want to hang with him in the TV room. You'll have to take Dolly and Leo after."

Dolly was a full brindle beauty. She was going to a foster family next week. And Leo, who was black and white, and lovable brute, had some adopters coming to see him on Monday. I'd miss him, but Parker had checked them out, and Leo was getting a great new forever home.

"Sounds perfect."

"Hey, Lily," Parker said.

I turned and gasped. It was the first time I'd seen him since the kiss. He wore a dark-blue suit that accentuated his broad shoulders and tapered waist, a pale-blue shirt, and a silver-and-blue striped tie that complimented his blue eyes. His hair was neatly trimmed and styled, and his five o'clock shadow was shaved clean. All my lady parts stood at attention.

"Wow, you look really nice."

He smiled, but it was tight. Not happy. "Thanks."

"You ready for tonight?"

"Yep."

Paul's eyes shined with humor. "I think this is the first time I've ever seen you in anything but jeans, T-shirts, or flannel."

"Me too," I said. "Naomi will be proud to have you next to her tonight. Any woman would."

"Any woman?"

I glanced at Paul. He clipped Addy on the shoulder. "Come on, kid. Let's get to work." The man knew how to take a cue.

"Thanks, Mr. Knowles," the teenager said. "You know, for giving me a chance."

"Sure, Addy. I'm happy to do it."

Paul and Addy took off, leaving Parker and me alone in the office.

Parker leaned against the wall but he didn't say anything. I could see the internal conversation going on in all the micro-tics happening in his face. I wished I could get inside his brain and hear his thoughts, but while I had good ears, they weren't that good.

I broke the silence. "I thought you might call last night."

"I almost did."

"What stopped you?"

"This." He looked me in the eye. "I can see it written all over you, plain as day."

"What?"

"You want to be friends. I get it." He stood up straight and pulled back his shoulders. "It's harder for me than for you. I'm not a dense man. I know when someone likes me. When you were in my arms the other night, I'd never felt anything so right. I know it wasn't just me."

I shook my head. "No, it wasn't just you."

"Then why do you keep putting roadblocks between us?"

Smooshie leaned hard up against my leg, as if she could sense my distress. "Because we're too different."

His ears reddened, and his lip curled at the corner. "What does that even mean?"

Inside, I said, *I'm not human, you are.* Out loud, I said, "You have to trust me."

"But I don't," Parker said. "I don't trust you at all."

I couldn't smell the lie behind his anger. He might trust me with the work, but he didn't trust me with his heart. It broke mine. "I'm sorry, Parker. I really am." I led Smooshie from the room, and we headed down the hall to hang with Tripod.

I heard the door to the office slam, and I winced as Parker left the building. I looked at Smooshie, who was giving me a *you blew it* look. She wasn't wrong.

Tripod—named because he only had three legs, one in the front, two in the back—hopped over when Smooshie and I walked into his room. Both pitties did the butt-sniff dance as they circled the floor. I sat down on the blanket-covered couch, and Smooshie jumped up on one side of me while Tripod managed to get up on the other side.

It was quiet in the room, so I turned on the TV. I needed noise to drown out my thoughts.

Why did Parker have to make things so difficult? I supposed he could ask the same thing about me. I wasn't *trying* to be difficult. On the contrary, I was trying to keep my life as simple as possible.

I focused my attention on the murder of Merl Peterson, because it was better than wallowing in self-pity.

What did I know?

Merl was a pillar of the community. He owned a lot of property around town. He had no wife or children. He left all of his estate to the Moosehead Lodge. He was bashed in the head on the college campus. There was no connection between Merl and the mummy formerly known as James Wright. James Wright wasn't from the area, but his partner Gail Martin used to live where James' body was found.

I shuddered. I couldn't believe the history behind that house. Well, at least I didn't have to worry that the family who "disappeared" in the eighties was buried in the floorboards or stuffed in the attic. That was a big relief.

The body had been in the wall less than a decade. Martin had been locked up thirty years ago. Why would Wright, twenty years or more later, go to Martin's childhood home? Nothing about this case made very much sense.

And what about the holes that were depressions on the property? Most of them looked pretty old, but some of them were fresher. While I suspected they were man-made, I hadn't discounted an animal, because Smooshie really did seem to think there was some exciting activity happening underground, but I found it hard to believe that an animal made all those impressions. When I'd looked at them from higher up, they'd formed a rough grid pattern. I knew gophers dug in multiple places around the same area, and that could give the holes a grid-like feel, but there was something too uniform about these. I wanted to talk to Jeff. He said he hadn't killed Merl, and my lie-detector didn't ping. Even so, he knew something about what was happening on my property, and if I could question him, I was certain I could get him to tell me the truth.

When Paul's shift ended, Addy came and found me. "Do you think I could stay and shadow you tonight as well?"

I remembered Nick had said that Addy was a quarterback for the football team. Why wasn't he going to his coach's party? "It's Saturday night. Don't you have the retirement banquet tonight?"

He blushed. "I'm grounded."

"What did you do?"

He toed the floor and wouldn't meet my gaze. "I got drunk with a buddy the other night, and things got a bit...stupid. Even for me."

The way he avoided looking at me, and his sudden desire to work here, made me wonder if the "stupid" involved a .22 rifle.

Before I could say yes or no, the teenager added, "Besides, working here tonight will give me something to do other than look at my bedroom walls. Dad's okay if I stay, and I really want to help."

The kid's eyes pled with me, and I didn't have the heart to turn him away. In many ways he reminded me of my brother Danny. It made me want to give him a chance.

"I don't mind, then," I finally said.

We took turns spending time with each dog. Smooshie was used to having the front office to herself, and she had a nice big pillow bed to plop down if she wanted. Besides, she'd dragged her favorite toy, a squeaky monkey, from the toy room, and hid it under the pillow bed. She liked to keep guard like a dragon sitting on treasure.

Around seven, Greer came in. "Your truck's going to be ready by tomorrow afternoon."

"You're the only garage open on Sundays," I noted.

"Technically, I'm closed tomorrow, but I got nothing better to do."

I asked Parker once why his father worked on Sundays. He told me it was his dad's way of pissing off God because God had pissed him off. I understood how loss could shake your faith.

Greer held up a thermos. "I brought some fresh coffee. Want a cup?"

"You don't have to ask me twice." We went into the office, and I grabbed two Styrofoam cups from near the empty coffee pot. I'd meant to make some, but it was easy to lose track of time here.

He poured and we both sat. "Helluva day," Greer said.

"Helluva week," I corrected.

"Ain't that the truth." He blew on his cup, steam rolling over the rim. "I'm just glad they got Merl's killer. I can't believe it's Jeff Callahan though. That boy, same as the others, always had so much respect for Merl. He used to hire them for this and that. Give them a little extra money."

"Parker said that. I'm really sorry again about your friend."

He stared down into his cup. "It's always hard. Open house is on Monday and the funeral is Tuesday. They finally released Merl to the funeral home this morning."

"You let me know if there's anything I can do to help, okay? You and Parker have been incredible to me. I don't know if I would have stayed if it wasn't for the two of you. And Buzz, of course."

"You've helped us too, Lily. In ways you can't even see." He smiled sadly. "We're both glad you ended up in Moonrise."

My phone beeped. I had a text from Nadine. "Hold on, Greer." I unlocked the screen.

Jeff had an alibi.

"Oh no."

"What is it?"

We had to release him.

"Callahan has an alibi. Apparently good enough they let him go."

Greer's nostrils flared. He clenched his fingers hard enough to crumple the Styrofoam cup full of hot coffee. "Son of a—" He shook his hand.

"We need to get cold water on that," I said. I set my phone down and unrolled some paper towels. I handed a wad to him.

He took them and dried his fingers. "I'm fine." Greer walked over the trash bin next to the desk. He glanced down at my phone. "What's that?"

"What?" I picked my phone up. I must have swiped the back button with my palm when I set it down, because the picture Reggie had sent me was on the screen. "Oh. You weren't supposed to see that."

"It's a weightlifting club medal."

I picked the phone up and enlarged the picture. "It says 400 on it. What does that mean?"

"It means the person who got the medal was able to lift 400 or more pounds."

"How do you know?"

"Parker had one. He actually had four of them— 200, 250, 300, and 350. The football coach gave them out when the boys hit their target goals."

The body had been in the wall for nearly seven years. Could one of Parker's high school friends have murdered James Wright? Maybe. But why kill Merl? I still couldn't quite make the connection.

I stared at Greer. I didn't want to tell him that the medal had been in James Wright's hand. Besides, I made a promise to Reggie. Even so, I had to find a way to warn Parker he might be partying with a killer right now. "I need to go. I have to talk to Parker."

"Finally come to your senses, huh?"

"What?"

"You and my boy belong together. He should be with you, not with Naomi."

I didn't want to mislead Greer, but I also didn't want to have to explain. "What about the shelter?"

Greer nodded. "I'll stay here and watch Smoosh and the other dogs."

"And Addy," I said. "Thank you." I winced. "Can I borrow your car?"

Greer pulled the keys to his coupe out of his pocket and handed them to me. "Don't ding her."

"I won't." I'd call Nadine on the way. The medal wasn't enough to arrest anyone. Especially if the whole football team had them. And it could have been from someone a little older or even younger. But I had my suspicions about the killer of both Wright and Merl, and I thought I'd finally figured out the why.

He touched my arm before I could put on my sweater. "Don't break his heart, Lily."

I hugged Greer. "Don't worry."

CHAPTER SEVENTEEN

I TRIED TO CALL Nadine, but her phone went to voice mail. I texted her: *Call me!* I nearly broke down and called the sheriff, but I doubted he'd believe my suspicions. Plus, I could get Reggie in a lot of trouble if Avery found out she'd sent me pictures of evidence. My heart raced in my chest, and my claws came out as I drove to Moonrise High School. I wasn't sure what I'd do when I got there.

The town was small enough that it only took five minutes to get to the school. The parking lot was packed. There had to be at least sixty or seventy cars, trucks, and vans sandwiched side by side. I parked near the road. I tried calling Nadine again. Straight to voice mail. I called Parker's number and got the same.

I rolled my shoulders to ease the tension. "Just get out of the car," I told myself. "One foot after the other." This was a fool's mission. The truth was, there probably wasn't going to be any trouble at the high school, regardless of who killed Merl or James. I wondered if my motives were pure or selfish. Did I just want to see Parker with Naomi? Had I used this flimsy evidence as a way to crash the party?

I was honest enough with myself to admit it was a possibility.

People would be safe as long as the murderer thought he or she was safe. Right?

A car pulled in a couple of spots down from me. I saw Ryan Petry on the passenger side. The driver was Paul Simmons. I relaxed a little. I needed a friendly face right now.

I started to get out of the car, but stopped when Ryan leaned across the front seat and kissed Paul.

Oh. Wow. I was a terrible detective. However, it explained a lot. I'd seen Ryan do a lot of flirting with women, but he never smelled of lust or arousal. Apparently, I'd been sniffing him around the wrong gender.

Ryan got out of the car. He stood there watching as Paul backed up and pulled out of the school. I opened my door and got out as well.

Ryan heard me and looked up. I gave him my best reassuring smile, but he looked stricken. I strolled over and took his hand. "Your secret is safe with me."

He squeezed my hand. "You want to go inside?"

That had been a quicker conversation than I'd expected. I didn't press him, though. It was Ryan's thing, and he could talk or not talk about it as he saw fit. "Yes, please."

A truck drove up when were got to the door. It parked almost sideways in a parking space. Jeff Callahan stumbled out of the cab.

"This is bad," I whispered.

"Why?" Ryan asked.

"Jeff was arrested and released today for Merl Peterson's murder. It's pretty clear he was framed, and—"

"Move out of my way," Jeff said. He bared his teeth as he shoved past Ryan and me.

"We have to stop him."

"There's a reason I'm a veterinarian and not a cop, Lily."

Exasperated, I sighed. "Fine. Then let's go find a cop. Nadine is in there somewhere."

When we got into the gym, the auditorium was decorated with streamers. A big banner with the team's picture, Coach Thompson on one end of the players and Assistant Coach Nick Newton on the other. The tables were covered with white cloths, sparkles, flower arrangements, and candles. There were men and women of all ages in attendance, but the coach had been around for a couple of decades. The current team, a group of about thirty teenage boys of various sizes. Addison should have been among them, but a grounding was a grounding.

All in all, the gym had been turned into a banquet hall. It was pretty. I took out my phone. No bars. Great. It was no wonder I couldn't get through to Nadine or Parker. Coach Thompson the 2009 team had attracted a huge crowd. The gym was wall-to-wall with people. The sea of folks milling around made it even harder to find my friends.

A woman stopped Ryan and me before we got too far.

"You need badges," she said. "Though I'd know Ryan Petry anywhere. You haven't changed a bit, Big Sexy."

Ryan flashed a charming smile and looked at the woman's name badge. "Celia," he said. "So nice to see you. You look great."

Celia beamed at his compliment. She rifled through the few names left on her table and grabbed Ryan's. "You didn't plus-one on your RSVP. I'm afraid I don't have a name badge for your friend."

"This is Lily Mason." He leaned in close to Celia. "You don't mind me bringing her in, do you? She's practically like my sister. You know how it is with family."

Once Ryan took me out of the she's-not-my-girlfriend equation, the woman giggled and gave us the go-ahead. Ryan offered me his arm. He looked handsome, stylish, and smelled really good. I looked disheveled, ready for a slumber party, and I smelled like dog. It was no wonder half the gym stared at us.

I finally saw Parker standing by Mark Stephens, Adam Davis, Nadine, Buzz, and a couple of other people I didn't recognize. Where the heck had Jeff Callahan gone?

"Parker!" I yelled. I was dressed in jeans and a black sweater. My tennis shoes gripped the gym's highly polished floor as I ran toward him. Ryan, who had no idea why I'd shown up, ran with me. He really was a good friend.

Parker's expression changed from surprised to pleased to pissed. Nadine saw me and just looked pleased. Good ol' Nadine. Parker needed to get over the whole Ryan thing. The only person who couldn't see that Ryan and I weren't interested in each other was Parker.

"Did you see Jeff?" I asked.

"No, why?" Parker said.

"He was arrested today for Merl's murder," Ryan supplied, stealing my thunder. "He was released and he just ran past us in here looking really freaked out."

"I told Parker about Jeff already," Nadine said, giving both Ryan and me a sour look. "And that we had to let him go. He had a solid alibi."

"I have some new information." I grabbed my phone from my purse and pulled up the picture. I showed it to Parker. Ryan moved around so he could see as well.

"I've seen that. It was in James Wright's hand when he died," Nadine said. "We don't know what it means yet."

The expression on both Parker's and Ryan's faces showed they both had a good idea what it was. "Who all had the 400 weightlifter medal on their jacket, Parker?"

His eyes were wide, his face incredulous. "There was only one guy who managed that kind of weight." He looked around. "Where's Adam?"

I searched the small crowd. The large man had been here moments before, but now, he was no where to be seen.

Nadine grabbed my arm. "Are you saying that pin belongs to Adam Davis?"

I looked at Parker.

Parker shook his head. "I can't know for sure, but Adam held the record in our weightlifting club. No one else got close to four hundred."

Nick Newton came over. "What's going on?"

"Have you seen Adam?" Parker asked him.

"He just went out the back door. I saw him go after Jeff." Nick gestured to the far side of the gym. "Something going on?"

"Jayzus," Nadine said. "If he killed Merl and tried to set up Jeff...I have to call for backup."

I showed her my phone. "No bars. I've been trying to call you both since I found out what the medal was."

"I'll go and check on them," Nick said. He walked away before Nadine could stop him.

"I'm going, too," Parker said. "If Adam framed Jeff, there could be trouble."

Nadine stepped in front of him. "You're not a cop, Parker. Let me handle this."

"I can handle myself." He pushed past her. I gave Nadine an apologetic look and took off after him.

Ryan started to follow, but Mark grabbed him by the arm as he glared at me. "What are you telling people, Petry?" Was this over the "Markles Sparkles"? Now that I knew Ryan was gay, it made me wonder if Mark and he had been more than friends in high school."

"Let go of me," Ryan said to him. "I never talk about you to anyone." He leaned in close to Mark. "I never even think of you."

That remark mostly confirmed my suspicion. Mark blinked, his face stricken. I waited as Ryan caught up to me.

"I'm sorry, Ryan."

"I am too," he said. "We better catch up if we're doing this."

I scanned the room and saw Parker heading out the back door. "There." Ryan and I took off in a sprint to the door Parker had exited.

****

The doorway led out to a concrete slab with a basketball hoop. On the other side, a green lawn and an equipment house. I saw Parker running toward the football field. He was shouting.

"Adam! Stop. You don't want to do this, man!"

Ryan and I picked up speed. There was a figure on the ground near the south-end goalpost.

Parker was there before us, of course, but it didn't take long for Ryan and I to get there. Parker had his hands pressed on Callahan's stomach. Blood oozed past his fingers as he tried to stem the flow.

"What happened?" I asked.

"Adam," Parker said. "He stabbed Jeff. I don't get it. Nick went after him, but I didn't want to leave Jeff. He's losing a lot of blood."

"Yes," Ryan said. I looked up. He was on his phone. "We have a stabbing victim at the Moonrise

High School varsity football field. South goalpost."
He paused as they asked the victim's name. "It's Jeff
Callahan. I'm Ryan Petry. Yes, we know who
assaulted him. No, he is no longer here or an
immediate threat."

While Ryan finished with the 9-1-1 call, I checked
Jeff's breathing and pulse. "Hang in there. Help is on
the way."

"You're in danger." Jeff blinked up at me. His
words were slurred.

"Don't speak," I told him. His lips were going
ashen, and his eyes kept shutting. Ryan had stripped
off his jacket and button-down shirt, then taken off
his T-shirt and handed it Parker to help hold pressure
and stop the bleeding.

Dang, he was in lean shape. He put his shirt and
jacket back on while I turned my attention back to
Callahan. "Why did he try to frame you for Merl?"

Jeff didn't answer.

I shook him. He blinked. "Why did he want you
to go down for Merl's death?"

"Money," Jeff hissed. "Wants the money."

"What money?" Parker asked.

"Adam wants the money?" I asked.

"No," Jeff said. "Not..." His eyes fluttered and
his respirations became labored.

"Tell me, Jeff. If not Adam, who?"

Jeff passed out from blood loss as sirens and lights flooded the end field. The emergency vehicles parked on the track nearest the end zone.

Nick came running back about that same time. He looked pale, and his breathing was labored.

Nadine ran to us, leading the charge. "Where's Adam?"

I shook my head.

Nick coughed, then took a deep breath. "He got away."

CHAPTER EIGHTEEN

PARKER DROVE ME home after we'd dropped off Greer's car at the shelter, he'd cleaned up and changed clothes, and we'd picked up Smooshie and Elvis. Elvis and Smooshie filled the backseat of his truck to capacity. Smooshie scratched at the window, hoping to ride with the wind in her face, but Elvis, the gray pittie-Great Dane mix, kept poking his head up into the front and setting his chin on Parker's shoulder.

There'd been so much blood. Parker looked numb and exhausted. His eyes reflected the night's horror. Nadine called and told us that Jeff was in critical condition, but the doctors were hopeful he'd make it. They still hadn't caught Adam. Jeff's words haunted me.

You're in danger, he'd said. But why? What was there left to hide?

"The money has to be the bank robbery money, right?"

Parker nodded, but said, "I don't know."

"What did you see when you saw Adam with Jeff?"

"Jeff was leaning against the goalpost. Nick was there, talking to them, but Adam was standing over Jeff, waving a knife at Nick. When I yelled, Adam took off." Parker flexed his grip on the steering wheel. "I still don't understand. Any of it," he clarified. "Adam and Jeff were best friends. He wouldn't hurt Jeff. Not the Adam I knew."

"He isn't the same man anymore."

Parker flipped on his brights when we exited onto BB road. "I can't believe he's changed so much."

"Haven't you?"

He gave me a quick unfriendly look then sighed. "I suppose I have. But he was still a teenager when that bank robber was killed. Why would Adam do that? And why kill Merl now?"

"Because Merl knew Adam put the body in the wall."

How could he?"

"You told me that Merl gave you your first job. Building decks, roofing, small home improvements, that kind of thing. I think Merl did the same with Adam." It was dark when we got to the trailer. I'd forgotten to turn on a light when I'd left. I looked at Parker. "Merl had called me when the body was discovered. He was angry when he hung up. We know he called Jeff, and Jeff probably called Adam."

"And he killed Merl to keep his secret."

"Exactly." I wondered if Adam was still a threat. The money had probably been found a long time ago by Jeff. I hadn't noticed any fresh dig spots on the property other than what Smooshie managed. If the guy had any sense at all he'd have escaped to Illinois or Kentucky by now. "I don't need you to stay, Parker."

Parker sat still, his fingers still gripping the wheel. He turned to me with hard eyes. "You heard Jeff. He said you were in danger."

"He'd lost a lot of blood. He was the one in danger, not me. Besides, Adam has no reason to come after me. The police are after him. His main focus will be his freedom." Besides, if Adam came around for me, I'd make sure he never tried to hurt me again. Meow. I couldn't do that if Parker was with me.

"I'm not leaving you, Lily. Not tonight."

In the distance, I heard gravel crunch beneath tires. "Someone's coming."

"I don't hear anything."

Crap. "I thought I heard something."

Parker turned off the truck engine and we got out. I gazed out into the darkness toward where I'd heard the vehicle.

"Do you see anything?" Parker stood behind me now. This close, I could feel the warmth of him. I stopped myself from purring.

"Goddess," I whispered, calling on her for strength. The full moon would be coming in the next week, and my control was a little shaky around lunar cycles.

Headlights flashed then went out.

"There it is," I said.

"That car had to be a good mile away, Lily. How did you hear it?"

"Must be the adrenaline," I lied.

A small white sedan pulled in. Parker stepped around me, placing himself between me and potential danger. But I could see in the car, and it wasn't Adam.

"Naomi," I said. Why was she here? It was eleven o'clock at night. "I don't have the energy to fend off her questions."

"I'll get rid of her," Parker said.

Too late though, Naomi was already out of the car and walking toward us.

"What are you doing here?" I asked.

"I..." Her normally shrewd expression faltered. She was still wearing a tight black dress that hugged her curves in all the right places. "I just want to ask a few questions."

"About what?" Parker growled.

I grimaced and sighed. "Naomi works for the *Dispatch*. She's a reporter."

"I know."

I looked at Naomi. "You've been trying to get me to talk about Bridgette Jones since you arrived. You're doing a story on the trial, aren't you?"

"Is that why you asked all those questions about Lily?" Parker's tone was livid. He clenched his fists.

"Yes," Naomi admitted. "My editor won't give me my own byline unless I can bring him something juicy. I thought the Tom Jones trial could be my big break. But there are nastier things going on in Moonrise right now, and I want this story. I *need* this story."

Naomi had tried to play at "hometown girl finds success in the city," but she was really a cog, trying to advance herself in a cutthroat world. I could smell the bitter scent of her desperation.

"You need to leave," Parker said. His voice was low and scary. "Now."

"Please. Just give me something."

How about a punch to the throat? My head began to pound as I worked to control my seething anger. I didn't care that she'd been trying to get a story from me. I did care that she'd used Parker. "Get off my property."

Her face pinched, and with crystal clarity, I could see a look of mortified interest. "What's wrong with your eyes?"

Stupid! I'd been careless. My eyes must have shifted, and the moon's light revealed the same glow other predatory animals had.

Parker turned to me. I closed my eyes and concentrated on keeping them human. "Go," he told Naomi.

She held up her phone, the light flashing bright as she snapped a picture of us.

I reacted. Badly. I closed the distance between Naomi and me with a single leap and swatted the phone from her hand. "Don't make me tell you again. Get off my property."

Naomi grabbed the phone from where it landed a few feet away and scrambled back to her car. I knelt down and took in deep breaths to calm my raging beast. So close. I'd come so close to exposing myself to both Parker and a persistent reporter.

Parker's hand was warm on my back. "She's not going to give up so easily," he said.

I hoped he was talking about her getting the scoop on the crimes, and not about trying to figure out why my eyes had looked so alien. "I agree. This isn't the last we've seen of her."

Parker went to the truck and let Smooshie and Elvis out. After, we went inside the trailer.

Even though I could see in the dark better than any human, I had a profound sense of relief to be indoors with the lights on. I sat on the couch. The two dogs sandwiched me on either side. Parker brought me a cold washcloth.

"I'm okay," I said. "You really don't have to stay. I'm sure Elvis would prefer his own bed."

"I told you I'm not going anywhere tonight." This time his tone was gentle, not angry and irritated like he'd been with me earlier.

The dogs jumped down from the couch and started barking. Parker went to the window. "There's a car pulling in, no lights."

I heard a quiet engine shut off. I'd been so focused on Naomi leaving, I hadn't heard the new car pull in.

Parker turned out all the lights in the trailer and locked the front door. "Stay down, Lily. We know Adam's dangerous."

"It might not be him."

"Then why turn the lights off and coast in?" He looked at me. "A noncombatant wouldn't have a reason to come in quiet."

"Adam's not a combatant."

The large man stepped out of his car. "I need that money, Lily. Don't make me come in there and take it from you," he shouted.

Why did he think I had the money?

Answering my unasked question, Adam said, "I know you've been digging around here. I don't want to hurt you, but I will." A loud blast followed by glass plates shattering in my cupboard where the bullet pierced the side of the trailer had Parker and me dropping to the floor.

"I can't get my life back without the money!" Adam sounded crazy and desperate. Not a good combination.

I stared at Parker, fear making my heart race and breath quicken. "I take it back," I whispered. "He's totally a combatant."

"Shhh." Parker crawled to the couch. He moved Smooshie and Elvis to the bedroom and slid the door shut. "Do you have a gun?"

"No," I hissed. I had other weapons, but none I could display in front of Parker.

Parker made his way toward the door.

"What are you doing?"

He put his hand on the door handle.

"No!" I whispered harshly. "Are you crazy? Don't go out there." The scent of my anxiety, like rotten citrus fruit, overwhelmed my senses. But Parker didn't stink of fear or trepidation. He had a calm about him I'd never seen.

It's combat, I thought. The storm comes after. I didn't know if it was reassuring or frightening that he seemed in his element.

He looked at me, his eyes shining with purpose. "Call the police."

I groaned. My fear had turned me into an idiot. I grabbed my phone and dialed.

"Nine-one-one, what is your emergency?" a woman asked.

Before I could answer, Parker opened the door. "No," I said. "Parker, don't."

"Hello," the operator said. "This is 9-1-1, do you have an emergency?"

The door closed. Goddess help me, I prayed. Why was Parker putting himself in danger? "There's a man with a gun outside."

"Are you in a safe place where you can talk, ma'am?"

I didn't feel safe, but I said, "As safe as I can get for now." Smooshie tried to crawl underneath me, smashing as much of her body against mine as possible. Crap. She was frightened. We both were. I really needed a Thunder Buddy vest, maybe two of them.

"Ma'am," the woman said again.

I went to the window and peeked outside. "I can't see them," I told her.

"Who?" the woman asked. "Tell me what's happening. Give me your location. I'll get the police dispatched to you right away."

"1031 northwest 400."

"Can you give me more information? Can you tell me your name?"

"This is Lily Mason." I went to the back window. Parker walked out from the shadows. My stomach gripped with fear for him.

"I'll take you to the money," he said to Adam.

"What the hell is he thinking?" I hissed.

"Who?" the operator asked.

Adam kept his gun trained on Parker. I let my eyes go cougar, and I could see his large hands were shaking. Please don't shoot him, I pleaded silently. My fangs dropped down and cut into my tongue as I pushed past the dogs in the bedroom and looked out the back toward the woods where Parker was leading Adam away. Away from me.

I saw the muzzle flash in the trees before the shot rang out. *Bang!*

"No!" I screamed. "Parker!"

"Lily," the operator said. "Lily. Tell me what's happening."

Dread clawed at my throat. "Another gunshot."

"Is anyone hurt?"

My skin tingled with goose bumps as a sudden chill took hold of me. "I don't..." I couldn't see anything more. The trees hid any movement. *Please, Goddess,* I bargained. *Not Parker. Not him.*

Renee George

CHAPTER NINETEEN

"ARE YOU STILL WITH me, Lily? The units on the way to you are fifteen minutes out. I need you to stay on the phone with me.

"I can't," I told the 9-1-1 operator. "I just can't." I had to help Parker. No matter what, no matter the cost. I couldn't lose him too.

Smooshie had stayed quiet and hidden since the gunshots, not that I could blame her, but now that I began to bark as she saw the beginnings of my shift. "No," I told her as I set down the phone. "Not this time, girl."

I made my way out of the trailer, hugging the front wall in a crouch, as I worked my way to the back end that faced the trees. I could see some movement. I stepped lightly, careful to not make a sound. There were some benefits to being a predator. I caught Parker's scent. I inhaled past the musty scent of wet bark and left over winter decay. Beyond that was I didn't smell blood. That was a good sign.

I pushed my beast forward, golden fur sprouting on my arms. Goddess help me if he saw me like this, but I had to use the only advantage I had at my disposal. I slipped quietly into the tree line, using shadows to hide my progress. I heard voice up ahead, and crept closer.

"Give me an excuse," I heard Parker say, his tone angry and menacing. "I'll blow your head off."

Relief flooded me. Parker had the gun. The upper hand. I pushed my beast back down, my skin returning to normal, as I raced toward his voice. I had a moment's relief when I saw Parker kneeling on Adam's back. He had the larger man's arms back, and with Adam's own shirt, Parker had trussed him up like a Thanksgiving turkey. The relief vanished when I saw he was holding a gun to Adam's head, his finger curled on the trigger.

"Parker," I said gently. "The police are on their way."

"He would have killed me," he said coldly. He pressed the gun tighter to Adam's head. "He would have killed us both."

Adam was crying, but he didn't move. "I didn't, Parker. I wouldn't."

I moved in next to him and went down to my knees in the dirt. "You stabbed your best friend."

"I'm not a killer," Adam said.

"Tell that to James Wright. To Merl Peterson." My hands began to shake. "You *are* a killer."

"The guy in the house. That was an accident," he sobbed. "I didn't mean to kill. We were working for Mills when we came on him in the woods. He had a gun. I didn't mean to hurt him."

"The shot to the head killed him. You'd already wounded the man. Why didn't you call the police?"

"I have a clear shot on your girlfriend, Knowles. You need to put the gun down."

From the back of the woods, Nick Newton walked out from behind a tree. He held a rifle up and pointed it in my direction. "Get up, Davis," he said to Adam.

"He's going to shoot me," Adam said, his face still sideways against the ground.

"No, he isn't. Are you, Parker?" Nick didn't waver with the rifle. He had the barrel trained on me.

I didn't know if I could dodge a gunshot, but I didn't want Parker to give in. "The police will be here anytime," I told Nick. "You won't get away with this."

Nick fired once, the bullet whizzing just above my head, and quickly chambered another round. "The next one is going to give you a third eye in that pretty forehead of yours." He tapped the trigger. "Now toss the gun and untie Adam. Don't make me tell you again."

Parker eased up with his gun hand and moved his knee off Adam. The larger man rolled away from him, getting himself loose from the T-shirt binding him. He put it on. I expected him to look angry, raging even, but Adam Davis still looked scared.

"Toss the gun," Nick demanded.

Parker looked at Nick, his eyes narrowed with disgust. He dropped the weapon.

"Pick it up," he told Adam.

Beast Mode Cowboy looked more like a lamb than a lion in that moment. He picked the gun up. "I'm sorry," he told Parker.

"Shut up," said Nick. "Let's go."

How did he plan on getting away with more murders? This was Moonrise, not Los Angeles. It wouldn't be too difficult for even Sheriff Avery to figure out this mess. Besides, the property would be filled with police in a few minutes. I could hear their sirens in the distance.

I walked to Parker when Nick lowered his rifle.

"There's no way out from here."

"There's always a way out." Nick gestured over his shoulder. "Come on. My truck is in the field behind your woods." His cruel smile made me shudder. "Didn't you know we were neighbors?"

Adam pointed the gun at us and said, "Move."

As we walked—Parker and I side by side, with Adam and Nick behind us—I tried to fit the puzzle together. "Adam fought with James Wright, and in the struggle the gun went off, wounding him." I glanced over and back at Nick. "But you shot him in the head."

"Quiet," Nick said. "No talking."

I knew he wouldn't do anything while we were still on the property. He seemed to want something. "Why kill him?" I mused. "Why not call the police?" I snapped my fingers. "The money. The money from the bank robbery was never recovered. You thought it was hidden here somewhere. And by all the holes in the woods, you think it's out here."

Nick snarled. He hit me in the back with the butt of the rifle. Parker turned, ready to lunge, but I caught his arm and warned him off with a quick shake of my head. Adam still had a 9mm trained on us.

"Merl hired you, Adam, and Jeff to work for Mills, didn't he? That's why you killed him," I said to Nick. I swiveled my eyes to Adam. He looked tense, but also relieved.

"Adam shot Wright in self-defense, but he told you about the money hidden on this land. So instead of turning him in, Nick, you got greedy."

Nick came up behind me and wrapped his arm around my neck. I tucked my chin and bit into his arm. He screamed and pulled the trigger on his rifle.

A dead silence followed a groan of pain as Adam slumped to his knees. Blood darkened his white T-shirt on the left side. He dropped the gun, gripping his chest.

Parker lunged for the weapon, but Nick threw me aside and had his rifle back up and pointed at Parker.

"No!" I screamed, and it came out like a mountain lion's roar.

I slashed at Nick, pouncing on his back. The big man swung at me with his rifle, another shot rang out. All my fear turned to fiery rage. This man killed Merl, and he would kill Parker and me if given the chance.

I wouldn't let him. I couldn't. I didn't care what it took to take him down.

The side of his gun hit me in the face. I jumped to my feet with inhuman quickness.

When Nick saw me for the first time since I'd first attacked him, he stumbled back with fright. He lifted his gun and aimed it at me. Parker shoved him from the side, but Nick managed to hang on to his weapon. He swung it at Parker like a baseball bat. Parker ducked, and when he did, I launched myself at Nick, tearing at his flesh with my claws. He screamed. And screamed. And then he didn't.

I fell to the ground when his body went limp beneath me.

Parker stared at me. His face white with shock and disbelief.

I'd lost control. I'd exposed my true self, and Parker would hate me for it. *I* hated me for it.

I shook my head. "I'm sorry, Parker. I tried…" I forced the fur on my arms to recede, and my fangs and claws to retract. Oh Goddess. I broke rule number one of living amongst humans. Never let them see you shift.

"What are you?" he asked. I took a step toward Parker, but he took a step back. His hand gripped the 9mm as if it were his lifeline. Would he shoot me?

"I've wanted to tell you for a while now. I—"

Barks and shouting, along with wide-beam spotlights, flooded the woods around us.

Sheriff Avery's voice boomed as he yelled out commands.

"Over here," Parker said. He gave me a look I couldn't read. I braced myself for whatever would happen next.

Smooshie and Elvis were the first to get to us. Elvis went right to Parker and put his head under Parker's hand. Smooshie, however, made a show of sniffing the bodies and examining the entire scene. I grabbed her by the collar to keep her away from the bloody gore.

Nadine, Morris, and another deputy came into the clearing with Avery. They had their guns up and pointed at us. "Drop the weapon, Knowles!" Avery said.

Parker bent at the knees and set the pistol on the ground. "Nick Newton killed Merl Peterson," he said. "He and Adam were planning to do the same to Lily and me."

I could tell Nadine wanted to get to me, to see if I was okay, but she also wanted to keep her job. I nodded at her. Some of her tension eased.

Avery looked suspicious. "So why are you two standing? And they're on the ground?"

Here it was. The moment of truth. How would Parker explain Newton's wounds? They were definitely not made by a human.

Parker stared at me for a moment, his facial expressions changing as he tried to work out what he would say. "It was dumb luck." He shrugged. "Damnedest thing. A bobcat jumped out of a tree at Nick. His rifle went off and shot Adam. The wild animal attacked him until he fell, and then took off."

Avery looked at me. My mouth was dry as I backed up Parker's story. "It's true. It came out of nowhere."

Nadine stood between Sheriff Avery and me. A shield of sorts. When he left us alone, she said, "Shortly before you called nine-one-one, Jeff

Callahan told us everything. The James Wright killing. The looking for the missing bank robbery money all these years. It was Nick that stabbed him, by the way, not Adam." Her mouth turned down in a frown, and her eyes reflected a sadness. "Adam had stopped Nick from finishing Jeff off."

"Well, that's something, I suppose." Not that it would do him any good now. But at least he'd had decency left in him.

Nadine wrapped a blanket around me as medics made their way to the bodies. "I'm so glad you're safe," she said, and hugged me tight.

"Me too." I looked over at Parker. He stared at me like I'd sprouted fur and grew a tail. Wait. That's exactly what had happened. Granted, the tail was small in my half form, but it had been there.

Would he keep my secret? Goddess, what about Buzz? He'd made a real life for himself here. Had I ruined everything?

Parker went with Deputy Morris back toward my trailer. I walked with Nadine and Smooshie, who, of course, had to stop by every tree and pee. I had to pull the clicker out of my pocket to get her away from the one that housed the gray squirrel family.

Maybe Haze would know a memory spell. She was so bad at witchcraft, though, she'd probably give him a magical lobotomy. I couldn't do that to Parker. Better I leave than to put him at any further risk from me.

It was several hours before the police presence went away. Parker left without saying goodbye. He hated me. Who could blame him? He'd faced a lot of enemies in his life, but he'd never come across a monster like me.

"You sure you don't want to come home with me?" Nadine asked.

"Yes, I'm sure." I didn't know how much longer I'd been in Moonrise, and I wanted to spend my last days and nights in my own place.

CHAPTER TWENTY

THE CLEAR BLUE sky and warm sun promised a beautiful day as I watched Smooshie chase butterflies in the yard. I'd spent several days hiding out on the property, trying to soften my depression with demolition in the house. I'd already torn out the wall upstairs between the two bedrooms. It had been easier than I thought it would be, and while Nick had been a brutal killer, he'd also been right about them not being load-bearing walls.

Buzz was still mad at me, and I couldn't blame him. He offered me hope in a way that felt like a punch to the gut. He told me that no matter what Parker said, people wouldn't believe him. Nobody else had seen me shift, so Parker would come off as delusional. Folks would assume his PTSD had gotten the best of him in a bad situation. No harm, no foul.

Only, it felt like a lot of harm. I didn't want Parker to suffer because of me. Just the opposite. My lack of control had been a direct result of him being in danger. Add to the fact that I'd never killed anyone before, and three days by myself was a lot when it came to rehashing the fight over and over in my mind.

I believed with all my heart that Nick Newton was going to kill Parker. As many times as I ran the scenario in my head, I knew without a doubt, if it came down to him being alive or me being outed as a Shifter, I'd choose getting outed every time.

Jeff Callahan recovered after emergency surgery. Nadine told me he had confessed everything: Adam's fight with Wright, Newton shooting Wright in the head then blackmailing both teenage boys into staying quiet. He told them they'd go down for murder with him, accessories to the crime. Nick also blackmailed Jeff into trying to find the money with him, and to also try to buy the property when it went up for auction. They'd both been responsible for the multiple holes. Adam had gone away to play football and hadn't returned. He'd almost believed he'd been out of it, but when he came home to honor his old coach, his worst nightmare had been waiting for him.

Nick made Jeff arrange a meeting with Merl then he killed him and set Jeff up for the murder when the police started poking around Merl's calls, which had included me and Nick. Jeff had been with Freda, though, when the murder went down.

Air-tight alibi. Freda had sat at his bedside almost constantly since his stabbing. She was nineteen years older than Jeff, but she was very attractive. Too attractive for Jeff Callahan. But who was I to judge. Jeff would be going to prison, so I hoped she wasn't too attached to the accountant.

Goddess, I hoped Jeff didn't take back his confession. I was already struggling under the weight of testifying at the Tom Jones trial.

They still didn't know who'd fired at my truck. And while I suspected it was Addison Newton, I didn't have any plans to rat the kid out. Frankly, I liked him, and not just because he reminded me of Danny. I wanted him to have a chance. I was just sorry I wouldn't be around to see it.

Parker hadn't called me or stopped by since the night I went all furry on him. I wanted to call him, but that wouldn't be fair to Parker. He had a right to be freaked out.

I hadn't called Hazel about the whole mess. I didn't want her trying to fix things for me. I would leave if it came down to it, for Parker and Buzz's sake. I didn't want to ruin either of their lives. But I would definitely miss the place. It already felt like home.

A gray squirrel sprinted across the yard. Smooshie barked, her interest in the butterflies lost, and took off in a race toward the woods with the small creature.

"Smooshie!" I ran after her as she followed the squirrel to the big oak with the hollow at the bottom. My pittie shoved her large head under the hood of the tree bark, her tail wagging as her nails bit into the dirt.

Renee George

I grabbed her collar and yanked her back. "No, Smoosh!" I grabbed her clicker from my pocket and snapped it like mad to get her attention. After a few seconds, she gave up, but her muscles were bunched with explosive energy, and I knew that if given half a chance, she'd burrow herself into the tree.

As I held her tight, I noticed tiny marks in a bare strip of bark on the exposed roots. I leaned down for a closer look. There was a tiny "x" etched into the wood, too precise to be an accident.

A rush of excitement warmed my skin.

I heard a vehicle coming up the drive, and recognized the sound of Parker's dually. My stomach lurched into my throat. I hurried to the edge of the woods. When Parker got out by himself, and not with a bunch of hunters or men in lab jackets, I shouted, "I'm down here."

He looked surprised then started walking down past the trailer to me. "You're not naked again, are you?"

My heart fluttered. His expression was cautious, pensive even, but his tone had been teasing. I stepped out so he could see me. "Fully dressed."

He half smiled. Smooshie ran to him, her whole body happy to see him in a way that only Smoosh could show. I was happy too, but after three days of nothing, I wasn't sure what to expect.

"Are you doing all right?" I asked.

Parker shoved his hands in his pocket. "Not really, but I'm also not *not* all right. If that makes sense."

"I'm really sorry, Parker. I wasn't trying to scare you."

He squinted at me, his lips thin and tight. "I saw what I saw. Right? You turned into something."

I could tell him no. Maybe try to convince him it was his PTSD that made him see things. A trick of his eyes. Would that be easier for Parker to cope with? Would he be content to believe the lie?

"I'm a Shifter." My pulse became a dull thud as heat climbed my skin. I'd faced killers, crazy magic, and I'd also been shot, but never had I felt so afraid. "A werecougar." I looked at him. His gaze met mine. "So you were close with the whole bobcat thing. Well, at least you were in the right family."

"This can't be real." He shook his head. "I've been trying to convince myself for the past couple of days that what I saw couldn't possibly have happened. How is this real?"

"There is a lot in this world that exists outside of human knowledge. The kind of magic and monsters that people only see in fiction and fairytales. It's overwhelming, even when you live in that world. Trust me. It's the reason I moved. I can't even imagine what it would be like to be a human with this knowledge."

"You're not human." He said it in a way that was pure statement, not a question. I could see the doubt creeping into his eyes.

"I'm not," I said. "Do you want to see?"

Slowly, he nodded. "Yes."

"Are you going to freak out?"

His Adam's apple bobbed. "Maybe." Smooshie stuck her head between my knees and I automatically petted her rump. "What about Smooshie? Does she…know?"

I smiled. "Yes. We run together."

"The other night, when you were naked?"

"Yep." The creep of blush warmed my cheeks. "I knew you wouldn't leave if I didn't show myself, so…"

"Oh." His blue eyes sparkled. "So are you going to get naked now?"

"Parker!"

He chuckled. It made me feel like maybe things would be okay. "I'm kidding." His expression turned serious. "Unless you really are going to get naked."

"How about if I just sprout some fur, maybe a couple of whiskers?"

He nodded, watching me with expectancy.

I took me a moment to get my concentration right. Talk about performance anxiety. Finally, my skin turned into a pale-golden fur, about the same texture as Smooshie's. A set of claws replaced my fingernails.

Parker's eyes widened. I waited for him to make the next move. Finally he said, "Can I touch...er, you?"

"Uhm, sure." I held out my hand.

He closed the distance between us with measured steps. He reached out, his hand hovering over mine. I imagined it was like getting up the nerve to touch a snake. When he stroked my fur, I swallowed hard. My throat had gone dry with heat and nerves.

"Soft," he muttered. He pressed the tip of his index finger to the point of a claw. "Sharp."

"This is beginning to sound like a *Sesame Street* episode." My words were breathy.

He looked at me, his blue eyes warmer than blue should be. "Lily," he said.

I went up on my tiptoes.

He stepped back. "I...I need a little time."

"Okay." I tried to keep my disappointment out of my tone. "No one can know about me. Not ever. It would be more than dangerous for my kind to get exposed as real."

"No one would believe me even if I was inclined to tell someone. Which I'm not."

"If you want me to leave, I'll leave. I don't want to complicate your life."

"Too late for that." He touched my chin. "Look. I'm asking for a little time here. That's all. I just found out the woman I love isn't quite human. I don't know how to process how I'm feeling right now."

I didn't either. Parker just confessed to being in love with me. "If you want time, I'll give you what you need."

"Well, right now, I need you to come back to work." He looked more relaxed now. "The dogs miss you, the volunteers miss you, and I miss you. Besides, Greer has your truck ready, and he says every day it's in his parking lot is lowering the property value of his garage." He smiled at me. "Besides, I'm going to be fundraising hard in the coming weeks. I want to get the new shelter built by the end of summer. It's going to take a lot of money. But nothing feels impossible when you're around."

Nothing's impossible. "The tree!"

"What?"

"Come on." I willed my fur back to skin and my claws to recede then grabbed his hand. I took him to the marked oak. After pulling Smooshie out again, I rolled onto my back at the hole and began to climb in.

"Did you hit your head the other night?" Parker asked.

I rummaged around in the dark, feeling around with my hand above my head until I found what I was looking for. I yanked it down, my hand slipping into a loop handle, and crawled out of the tree.

"Is that what I think it is?" Parker asked.

The bag was a heavy canvas, dirty and moldy, but still intact. There was a lock at the top, but it had been exposed enough to the elements that I was able to tear at the fabric.

Inside were bricks of plastic-wrapped cash. Gail Martin's retirement plan.

I held up a square of one hundred dollar bills.

"We can't keep it," Parker said.

Goddess, I loved an honest man. "I wouldn't dream of it, but I think the finder's fee is ten percent." I put it in his hand. "That's about one hundred and fifty thousand dollars."

"You could do a lot with that, Lily. You could make your home the way you want it."

"Well, I could do that with my half."

He tucked his chin.

"You were here when I found it, Parker. That means we're partners. Fifty-fifty. Do you think seventy-five grand will get the new shelter off the ground? If not, I'll donate my half."

Parker put the cash back in the bag. He moved close to me. "Partners," he said. "You've got a deal."

And then he kissed me, his mouth moving gently against mine.

I didn't shout "woo hoo!" but I wanted to. I didn't know what the future would hold for Parker and me, but for the first time in three days, I had a lot of hope.

The End

Paranormal Mysteries and Romances
By Renee George

Peculiar Mysteries
www.peculiarmysteries.com
You've Got Tail (Book 1)
My Furry Valentine (Book 2)
Thank You For Not Shifting (Book 3)
My Hairy Halloween (Book 4)
In the Midnight Howl (Book 5)
My Peculiar Road Trip (Magic & Mayhem)
Furred Lines (Book 6)

Barkside of the Moon Mysteries
www.barksideofthemoonmysteries.com
Pit Perfect Murder (Book 1)
Murder & The Money Pit (Book 2)
The Pit List Murders (Book 3)

Witchin' Impossible Mysteries
www.romance-the-night.com
Witchin' Impossible (Book 1)
Witchin' Impossible: Rogue Coven (Book 2)
Witchin' Impossible: Familiar Protocol (Book 3)
Witchin' Impossible: Mr. & Mrs. Shift (Book 4)

About the Author

I am a USA Today Bestselling author who writes paranormal mysteries and romances because I love all things whodunit, Otherworldly, and weird. Also, I wish my pittie, the adorable Kona Princess Warrior, and my beagle, Josie the Incontinent Princess, could talk. Or at least be more like Scooby-Doo and help me unmask villains at the haunted house up the street.

When I'm not writing about mystery-solving werecougars or the adventures of a hapless psychic living among shapeshifters, I am preyed upon by stray kittens who end up living in my house because I can't say no to those sweet, furry faces. (Someone stop telling them where I live!)

I live in Mid-Missouri with my family and I spend my non-writing time doing really cool stuff...like watching TV and cleaning up dog poop.

Made in the USA
Columbia, SC
25 May 2020

98288099R00143